I0687054

THEY RODE TOGETHER

TOGETHER

BOOK SEVEN IN THE LANDON SAGA

A SOLSTICE WESTERN

TELL COTTEN

1

They Rode Together

Tell Cotten

Also by Tell Cotten

(The Landon Saga books)
Confessions of a Gunfighter
Entwined Paths
Cooper
Rondo
Yancy
Lee

Dedication
To my grandparents, Melvin and Carol

Illustrator: Bill Olivas
www.billolivas.com
wbolivas@yahoo.com

Cover design:
Marcy Meinke/Converse Printing & Design
www.ConversePrinting.com
mike@converseprinting.com

Solstice Publishing - www.solsticepublishing.com

Author's note

THEY RODE TOGETHER has a few continued storylines from previous books in The Landon Saga series. While it can be read as a stand alone, it is recommended that new readers start with the first book in the series, CONFESSIONS OF A GUNFIGHTER.

Part 1
"New Developments"

Chapter one

When he first spotted it, it was nothing more than a glimpse of something in the far distance. He squinted his eyes and could make out a brown lump on the ground.

Whatever it was, it wasn't moving.

Curiosity got the best of him, and he nudged his horse forward.

As he got closer he could tell that it was a flipped over wagon. A wheel had come off, and the axle was broken.

He scratched his jaw in thought. Then, he stood in his stirrups and studied the countryside in all directions.

He was several miles west of Huntsville, Texas. The terrain was mainly wide-open, with a few rolling hills and some trees.

He saw nothing suspicious, so he dismounted, tied his horse to the wheel, and circled the wagon.

As suspected, there were tracks leaving the wagon. Two horses, and one human on foot.

He knelt by the human tracks and studied them carefully. Judging from the size and stride, he figured a woman had made the tracks. She had also been running; probably chasing after the horses.

There was nothing of value in the wagon, so he untied his horse and stepped into the saddle. The tracks were easy to follow, and he trotted with ease.

It was a warm afternoon, and sweat trickled down his face.

It was only a slight annoyance. He was comfortable in the heat, and was accustomed to long days in the saddle.

A few hours passed, and by now the woman's tracks had slowed considerably. He could tell that she was beginning to drag her feet some, and he grinned wolfishly.

The tracks climbed a small, steep hill. He loped his horse to the top and stopped abruptly.

8

The woman was at the base of the hill. She had apparently passed out, for she was lying facedown on the ground; her arms sprawled out in front of her in her attempt to brace herself as she fell.

With his hand resting on the butt of his Colt, he encouraged his horse forward. He stopped beside her and studied her still form.

His curiosity grew when he noticed the striped prison clothes she wore. She was also young and had long, blond hair.

"Hey!" He said abruptly.

She didn't stir.

"You dead?"

Still nothing.

Keeping an eye on her, he dismounted, tied his horse to a nearby bush, and approached her.

He nudged her in the ribs with the toe of his boot. There was a slight moan, and he nodded to himself.

"Well, you're alive," he said.

He started to turn back towards his horse, and that's when he spotted the rifle. She was lying on top of it, with the barrel pressed against her face.

An amused look crossed his face. He squatted beside her, reached underneath her stomach, and pulled out the rifle. She made a slight whimper, but that was all.

He stood, worked the lever several times, and emptied the rifle. The first shell that came out had been spent.

"Who have you been shooting at?" He wondered out loud. He thought on it and added, "Well, long as you ain't shooting at me, I don't reckon it matters."

He started to take the rifle, but then decided against it. He leaned it on a log that was close to her, gathered the shells, and walked towards his horse.

9

Chapter two

She woke with a soft groan. Her neck and back ached, and her head throbbed.

She grimaced as she took in a big breath. The smell of campfire smoke hit her, and she also smelled food. Her stomach growled uncontrollably.

She licked her cracked lips and forced her eyelids open. Then, she raised her head, blinked several times, and looked around.

It was evening time, and the afternoon heat had cooled considerably.

There was a campfire in front of her, and there was also a man sitting across the fire. A coffee pot was cooling to the side of the coals, and salt pork sizzled in a pan.

He was watching her with cold, calculating eyes.

"Hungry?" He asked.

"Yes," she said quickly.

"Figured you would be."

She rolled over into a sitting position. As she did, she spotted her rifle. She thought about grabbing it, but decided against it. Instead, she studied the man sitting before her.

He had a leathery face with a hard jaw. He was a tall man, and despite the smirk on his face, there was no kindness in him. He wore a Colt on his hip, and he looked comfortable wearing it.

"Who are you?" She asked warily.

"Rock Bullen," he replied, and added, "I'm a bounty hunter."

Her face stiffened.

"Bounty hunter?"

"Sure," he nodded. "I track down outlaws, kill them, and take them to the law and get paid for it."

She blinked as she thought on that.

"Do you always kill them?"

"Mostly."

"Why?"

"It's easier."

"I'm not an outlaw," she declared.

A wolfish grin split his lips.

"So you're just wearing those prison clothes for looks."

"I was in prison," she admitted. "But I was pardoned."

"Sure you was."

"You don't believe me?"

"Let's ride back to Huntsville and see what they have to say," Rock suggested.

She was quiet, and Rock chuckled sarcastically.

She eyed her rifle again. She glanced back at Rock, and he was watching her curiously.

"Are you the sort?" He asked.

"What sort?"

"Sort that would kill."

She pinched her face in displeasure.

"What an unpleasant question to ask," she replied, and added, "Besides, I'm sure you've already unloaded my rifle."

Rock's white teeth shone at her as he grinned.

"Smart girl."

She took in a big breath and sighed.

"So, you do this bounty work for money?" She tried to sound pleasant.

"Pretty much."

"How much do they pay you?"

"Depends."

"On what?"

"How bad they are. More people they kill, the higher the reward."

"I haven't killed anybody."

"We'll see."

11

"I was only in prison because I helped my husband escape from jail," she said truthfully. "There's probably not much reward for that, is there?"

"You always talk this much?"

"I know someone who would pay double any reward for me," she pressed on.

"Is that so," Rock chuckled, but not humorously. "And who would that be?"

"Ike Nash," she declared. "My name is Lucy Nash. I'm Ike's daughter-in-law."

Surprise showed in Rock's face as he stared at her.

Almost everybody in Texas had heard of Ike Nash.

He was known for being a shrewd and cunning businessman. He owned several ranches all across Texas, and he was involved in several businesses, mostly illegal. However, Ike had it set up so that nothing could be traced back to him.

"Take me to him," she continued. "I promise you that you will be well paid."

Rock didn't reply, and Lucy waited patiently.

"If you're who you say you are," he finally said, "what are you doing out here?"

Her mind raced.

"I was on my way home," she lied, "when two outlaws tried to jump me. I managed to lose them, but then the wagon flipped."

"Two outlaws?"

"That is correct. I recognized them too. Lee Mattingly and Brian Clark."

Again, Rock was startled.

"Lee and Brian? You're sure?"

"I've seen them before," she confirmed. "They are horrible, brutal men. If they had caught me there's no telling what appalling things they might have done."

"Appalling?"

12

"But then you found me," Lucy's eyes shone at him. "And I don't have to worry anymore."

Rock made a grunting sound, and he pinched his face as he thought on it.

"Lucy Nash," he finally said.

"That's me."

"You'd better not be lying."

"Of course not."

It fell silent again. Rock just sat there looking thoughtful, and Lucy's stomach growled.

"I believe that salt pork is ready," she finally suggested.

Rock looked sharply at her, and she smiled coyly.

Chapter three

It took several weeks for Rock and Lucy to reach Ike's ranch headquarters.

A lot happened during that time.

Ike Nash was now dead, killed by Lee Mattingly and Brian Clark. They also rode to Empty-lake and killed a politician named Ron Gallegan. After that they left town and hadn't been seen since.

Butch Nelson rode to town a few days after the killings.

Empty-lake was mostly a cow town of some two-dozen buildings. Two establishments stood out the most. The sheriff's office built by the late Lieutenant Porter, and The Palace Hotel, currently owned by Jeremiah Wisdom.

This was the first time since Ike's death that Butch had left the ranch. It had been a stressful time, and this was a welcome distraction.

Butch had been Ike's right hand man. He was attempting to keep Ike's business affairs going, but most of Ike's men were still undecided on whether to stay or go.

It didn't help that Butch was such a plain looking man. Short with a broad face, he looked more like a storekeeper.

But he was far from that. He was very good with a Colt, and he always displayed one on his hip. However, even with the Colt, there was still nothing that really stood out.

As Butch rode down the street, he spotted sheriff Rondo Landon and his deputy Ross Stewart.

They were sitting on the porch at the jail, drinking coffee and studying a chessboard. Rondo looked pleased, but Ross was muttering to himself.

Rondo looked up and spotted him, and his face sharpened in curiosity. He nodded, and Butch returned the nod.

He felt Rondo's eyes on him as he walked his horse down to The Palace Hotel. He dismounted, tied his horse to the hitching rail, stepped up onto the porch, and walked through the batwing doors.

He stood to the side as his eyes adjusted, and then he looked around.

The floors were clean, the bar shined, and all the glassware shone. There was also an enticing aroma coming from the kitchen.

Butch smiled his approval. It appeared as if Jeremiah Wisdom was doing a fine job.

Jeremiah was tending bar. Butch caught his attention, and Jeremiah gestured at the poker room.

Butch nodded and walked to the back.

There was only one man in the poker room, and he was seated at a table eating breakfast.

Butch studied him as he walked over.

He was dark headed with a thin and frail frame. He had quick, shifty eyes, and he also had large upper teeth that showed most of the time.

The man heard him approaching, and he smiled and stood.

"Are you Butch Nelson?"

"I am," Butch said as he stared at his teeth.

"You got my message?"

"That's why I'm here."

He nodded, sat back down, and gestured at a chair.

"Join me for breakfast?"

"I already ate."

"I see. How about a drink?"

"All I want is to know why you sent for me," Butch said, and there was a stern warning in his voice.

The man didn't seem rattled.

"Of course," he nodded. "I'll get right to the point then."

"That would be good."

"My name is Ed Hazel," he introduced himself. "I was Ron Gallegan's personal assistant."

Butch blinked as he thought on that.

15

"The politician that Lee Mattingly killed?"

"That's right. He and Ike were friends."

"Yes, I know that."

Ed smiled politely.

"Would you like to join me now?"

"I'll see what you have to say," Butch said as he eased into a chair.

"Our bosses were very successful business partners," Ed announced, and asked, "Did you know that?"

"I knew they had an agreement of some sort."

"That's all you know?" Ed frowned.

"Ike kept his business affairs mostly private," Butch explained.

"But he trusted you?"

"I think he did."

Ed nodded, satisfied. He took a swig of coffee and wiped his mouth with a napkin. Butch meanwhile, stared at his teeth.

"Did Ike ever mention the railroad?" Ed finally asked.

Butch thought for a moment.

"Not that I can recall," he said.

"But you're the one who, ah, *bought* all of Ike's ranches for him."

"I was," Butch nodded.

"Didn't you ever wonder why Ike was buying ranches all over Texas?"

"It wasn't my job to wonder."

"Ike was very particular on which ranches he wanted," Ed continued.

"I noticed that."

"That's because Ron Gallegan was telling Ike which ranches to buy," Ed informed.

"How come?" Butch narrowed his eyes.

Ed leaned forward in his chair. There was still nobody else in the room, but Butch couldn't help but lean forward too.

16

"It's still a few years away, but the railroad is coming to Texas," Ed announced in a hushed voice. "There's already a railroad committee mapping out the routes, and Ron Gallegan was on that committee. He was Ike's informant."

Butch frowned thoughtfully but didn't say anything.

"Don't you realize what this means?" Ed asked, and then he answered his own question. "After the railroad comes, there won't be anymore cattle drives going to Kansas. Instead, beef will be shipped back east straight from Texas. There will also be new settlers and new towns."

Ed let this sink in for a moment. He took another swig of coffee, wiped his mouth, and looked back at Butch.

"The railroad will also have to pay passage," he said softly, and added, "Whoever owns that land will become extremely wealthy."

Butch nodded slowly as he started to understand.

"There's only one ranch we still need," Ed continued. "And it's an important one. Are you familiar with Midway?"

"Some."

"There's a rancher there named J.T. Tussle. He controls almost all of the range around Midway."

"I've heard of him," Butch said, and added, "He's a salty character. He won't sell."

"But he has to," Ed urged. "The railroad has big plans for Midway. It's the midpoint between El Paso and Dallas."

"He'll fight," Butch warned.

"But you have a lot of men," Ed objected.

"They aren't my men yet."

"But they haven't left?"

"Not yet."

Ed nodded. It was silent for a moment, and then he asked, "What's going to happen to all of the land that Ike owned?"

17

"I have a man named Bob Sprutt who can do forgery," Butch replied. "He's in the process of muddying up the records."

"Is he good?"

"He says he is."

"That's fine," Ed nodded. He hesitated and asked, "So, can you and I work together?"

"I think we can," Butch nodded slowly.

Ed grinned, and his teeth showed even more.

"What about Tussle?" He asked.

"I'll talk with the men," Butch replied. "If they agree, we'll head for Midway."

"Good," Ed looked pleased.

Chapter four

When Butch got back to the ranch, there was a strange horse tied to the hitching rail.

He narrowed his eyes as he wondered who it might be. He dismounted, tied his horse next to the other horse, and stepped up onto the porch.

Bob Sprutt met him at the door.

He was a tall, thin fellow with blue eyes and light hair. He was good with a Colt, and he was also keen and educated.

"How's the forgery coming?" Butch asked.

"Slow."

"What's the holdup?"

"Nothing much. It just takes time."

Butch scowled and grunted in response.

"There's a man and a woman waiting in the study," Bob changed the subject. "They want to see Ike."

"Oh?" Butch shot him a questioning look.

"I didn't tell them anything."

"Good," Butch replied, and asked, "Who are they?"

"Never saw them before."

Butch nodded. He checked his Colt and walked down the hallway.

The study had been Ike's favorite room in the house. It was where he had spent most of his time, scheming and planning his business affairs.

Even though Ike had been dead for weeks, there was still the faint scent of cigar smoke in the room. There was a cowhide spread out in the middle of the floor, a fireplace in the corner, and a fancy desk next to the window.

The man and woman were seated in front of the desk. They stood when they heard him.

The man was tall and wide and looked mean, but Butch paid him little attention. Instead, his eyes grew wide as he stared at the woman.

"Hello, Butch," she smiled warmly at him as if they were old friends.

"Lucy Wells," Butch said blandly.

"No, Lucy Nash," she corrected.

They were both filthy and stank. Lucy's hair was a mess, and the prison clothes she wore were worn and had holes.

"You look good, Butch," she said pleasantly.

"You look horrible," he replied bluntly.

She smiled.

"I really mean it, Butch. You look good."

"I mean it too," he said as he continued to stare at her. "You look horrible."

"We've been traveling," she explained. "I haven't had a bath in weeks."

"I can tell."

Lucy smiled again, as if they had just exchanged a private joke. Nobody spoke, and several awkward seconds passed.

"What are you doing here, Lucy?" Butch finally asked.

"Where's Ike?" She asked as she ignored the question.

"You haven't heard?"

"Heard what?" Lucy asked, her eyes wide.

Butch didn't answer. Instead, he turned his eyes to Lucy's companion, and they studied each other.

"Who's this?" Butch asked.

"This is Rock Bullen," Lucy introduced. "He rescued me."

"Captured," Rock corrected in a gruff voice. "I captured you, not rescued."

Lucy shrugged, as if it made no difference.

"I told Rock that Ike would pay him handsomely for bringing me here," she informed Butch.

20

"Why would Ike do that?" Butch looked curious.

Lucy tried to look insulted.

"Because I'm his daughter-in-law!"

A thought suddenly occurred to Butch, and he nodded slowly.

"You are, aren't you," he said.

"So, where is Ike?" Lucy demanded.

"Dead."

Lucy and Rock were startled.

"Dead!" Lucy exclaimed. "What happened?"

"Lee Mattingly killed him."

"Oh, that *man*!" Lucy cried, and her eyes flashed in anger.

Rock grunted his displeasure. He turned abruptly towards Lucy, grabbed her arm, and pulled her towards the door.

"Let's go," he said gruffly.

"Where to?" Lucy demanded as she pulled back.

"See about a reward."

Lucy protested, but Rock paid her no mind as he dragged her along.

"Hold on," Butch said quietly.

"Don't try to stop me," Rock shot him a warning glance.

"How much of a reward were you hoping for?" Butch asked.

"As much as I could get."

"I see," Butch replied, and added, "I need to talk to Lucy."

"You going to pay the reward?"

"Perhaps."

"Why?"

"That's my business," Butch said.

The room was silent as Rock thought on that, and he shrugged and nodded.

"All right," he said as he released her arm. "Talk all you want."

21

"*Alone*," Butch frowned at him, and then he raised his voice. "Bob?"

Footsteps sounded in the hallway, and Bob appeared in the doorway.

"Yes?"

"Take our guest to the kitchen and fix him a cup of coffee."

Bob nodded and turned to leave, but Rock didn't move. He narrowed his eyes in suspicion as he studied them.

"Go on," Butch growled. "She's not going anywhere."

"She'd better not," Rock warned.

Butch forced a smile and nodded. Rock didn't like it, but he still turned and followed after Bob.

Chapter five

Soon as they were alone, Lucy rushed over to Butch.

"Please, Butch, *please*. I'll do anything, just help me!"

She stank even worse at close range, and Butch wrinkled his nose and stepped back.

"I might have a business proposition," he said. "But that's all."

"Yes, Butch?" She looked eagerly at him.

He cleared his throat and told her about the railroad and his arrangement with Ed Hazel.

"I'm in the process of muddying up the records; trying to get all of Ike's property in my name," he finished. "But, that might not be necessary now."

"And why is that?"

"You're Ike's daughter-in-law, his closest kin," Butch pointed out.

"You mean *I'm* going to inherit all of Ike's property?" She asked, and there was rising excitement in her voice.

"*If* I allow it."

Hope filled her face, and she smiled warmly at Butch.

"You know I've always been very fond of you, Butch."

"Have you now?" He raised an eyebrow.

"I think we would work really well together."

"Perhaps."

"What exactly do you have in mind?" She asked.

"We'll use your name, but it'll be my operation," Butch said. "I'll have final say in all matters."

"Of course, Butch."

"I've never been greedy. We'll split any profit right down the middle."

"That's more than fair. Oh Butch, I'm so excited!"

"You try and double cross me, and you'll be sorry," Butch warned.

Lucy tried to look hurt.

23

"I would never!"

Butch grunted and said, "All right. I'll pay Rock whatever he wants."

He headed towards the door, but Lucy stopped him.

"We might have a problem," she said.

"What's that?" Butch stopped and turned towards her.

"There probably is a reward out for me."

"How come?"

"I escaped from Huntsville," she admitted, and she explained all that had happened.

Afterwards, Butch sighed and shook his head.

"Yes, that might be a problem," he muttered.

"Couldn't I just change my name?" Lucy looked desperate. "After all, not many folks know who I am."

Butch's face lit up.

"Yes, that might work."

"I had a sister," Lucy offered. "She died when we were young. Her name was Jenny."

"I'll mention it to Bob, and see what he can do," Butch said.

Lucy looked pleased, but then her face turned dark again.

"We might have another problem," she said.

"What now?" Butch raised an eyebrow.

"Lee Mattingly and Brian Clark," she explained. "They were there when I escaped."

Butch scowled and then sighed.

"Those two really get around," he muttered.

"I want them killed," Lucy suddenly declared, and her eyes flashed in anger.

Butch was surprised by her boldness. He studied her for a moment, and he nodded slowly in agreement.

"Probably be best," he said, and asked, "Is there anything else?"

"Rock needs to be taken care of too," Lucy said matter-of-factly. "He knows too much."

"Is there anybody you *don't* want killed?" Butch stared at her.

"You, of course," she smiled.

"I'm glad to hear you say that," Butch said, and asked, "Any suggestions on how we go about this?"

Lucy frowned. It was silent for a bit, but then excitement filled her face.

"Why don't we hire Rock to go after Lee and Brian?" She suggested. "After all, he *is* a bounty hunter, and they *are* outlaws."

Butch was amused by the thought.

"Think Rock could do it?"

"Yes."

"Still, even if he caught them, he might not kill them."

"No," Lucy disagreed. "He told me that he always kills his prisoners. Said it was easier."

"He didn't kill you," Butch pointed out.

Lucy smiled.

"I'm different."

"Yes, you are," Butch agreed, and asked, "What about Rock? How do we take care of him?"

"We can worry about him later, after Lee and Brian are dead."

"You make it sound so easy," Butch smiled, and added, "All right. I'll talk to him."

He started towards the door, but Lucy reached out and grabbed his arm. Her grip was firm, but then it softened.

"Are partners in business all we can be?" She asked gently.

Again, Butch was startled, but he managed to conceal it. He stared at her for several seconds before he firmly pulled his arm away.

"You should take a bath before you try to be romantic," he suggested wryly.

Lucy scowled at him as he left the study.

25

Chapter six

Rock followed Butch back into the study. He held a cup of coffee and was also chewing on a biscuit.

"Have a nice talk?" He asked sarcastically.

Butch strode over to Ike's desk. He sat with authority, and Lucy stood behind him, looking proud.

Rock's face showed slight amusement as he watched them.

"I'd like to offer you a job," Butch announced.

"Doing what?"

"Lee Mattingly and Brian Clark. You know who they are?"

"Sure. Everybody does."

"I want them dead – I mean – captured. Both of them."

Rock narrowed his eyes. He glanced at Lucy, took a swig of coffee, and looked back at Butch.

"Why?"

"Doesn't matter," Butch replied. "Just give me your answer."

"First I'd ask about the price."

"Name it," Butch waved a hand at him, and added, "You can also collect any reward."

"Reward?"

"Sure. Lee killed a politician."

"I didn't know that," Rock said. He thought on it and asked, "What about the local law? What are they doing about it?"

Butch snorted in disgust.

"Rondo Landon is the sheriff, and he and Lee are close friends. He won't do anything."

"Interesting," Rock scratched his jaw. "I wonder if Rondo knows where they went?"

"He might, but he won't tell."

Rock smiled, but didn't reply.

26

"So, do you want the job?" Butch asked.

"Sure."

"Good," Butch nodded and stood. "Now, how much do I owe you for bringing Lucy home?"

Rock named a price. It was high, but Butch didn't argue. He got the money from the safe and paid him.

"By the way, nobody needs to know about Lucy being here," Butch said.

Rock looked unconcerned as he folded the bills and put them in his shirt pocket.

"I won't tell anybody."

"Make sure you don't," Butch said.

"Think I'll ride into town and stir up a little trouble," Rock changed the subject, and asked, "Is there a town council?"

"Yes. Last I heard, there were three members."

"What are their names?"

Butch told him, and Rock nodded.

"I'll start there," he said.

Rock put down his coffee cup, and without another word he walked out of the study. His footsteps sounded down the hallway as he went outside.

Butch walked over to the window. Lucy joined him, and they watched as Rock climbed on his horse and trotted towards town.

"Well, that's that," Butch said.

He glanced at Lucy, and she smiled back at him.

"I'm so excited!" She exclaimed.

"Yes, I imagine you would be."

"Could somebody fetch me some hot water?" She asked as she turned from the window. "I'd like to take a bath now."

"I'd appreciate that," Butch said truthfully.

27

Chapter seven

Butch told Bob to assemble the men, and they gathered in front of the main house after supper.

Lucy followed Butch out onto the porch. She was clean now, and her appearance had changed for the better. She wore an attractive dress, and everybody couldn't help but stare at her.

Butch got everyone's attention, explained the overall scheme, and then mentioned J.T. Tussle.

"Tussle is a salty character," Sim Hains, a tall, thin, and older man that most of the others looked up to, spoke up.

"He is," Butch agreed. "That's why we're going to kill him right off."

The men were startled by Butch's boldness.

"Why's that?" Sim asked.

"He'll never sell," Butch reasoned. "But, his niece Jessica might. Especially under the right conditions."

"What conditions might that be?"

"Tussle is preparing to make a cattle drive up to Kansas in a few weeks," Butch explained. "But, if he's dead and we take the herd, Jessica might be willing to sell."

The men were silent as they thought on that. They glanced at each other, and then they looked at Sim to speak for them. He nodded and cleared his throat.

"What's in it for us?"

"You boys can have the herd," Butch said. "Those yearlings will be worth a lot of money in Kansas."

"How many head?"

"Couple thousand, give or take."

Sim smiled wolfishly.

"That's a big herd."

"And they're all yours. All we've got to do is run them off and kill Tussle. What do you say?"

28

Sim glanced around at the men. They all seemed eager, so he turned back to Butch and nodded.

"When do we leave?"

"Sun up."

"We'll be ready," Sim said.

***

Everybody was up early.

After breakfast they gathered enough provisions to last a few weeks, and they packed down three mules with the supplies. Next, they saddled their horses, and they cut out a few extra horses to take along in case a horse went lame.

Butch tightened his cinch, climbed on his horse, and trotted over to Lucy, who was watching them from the porch.

"Three of the older men are staying," he told her. "They'll take care of things and help you if you need anything."

"Thank you, Butch."

"Bob is staying too. He'll work on changing your name."

"That sounds wonderful."

"Until I get back, I don't want you going into town. You could get into trouble if someone recognized you."

"I'll stay right here on the ranch," Lucy promised.

"Good," Butch nodded.

"How long will you be gone?"

"Hard to tell," Butch shrugged. "As long as it takes, I guess."

"And what am I supposed to do while you're gone?"

Butch made a wide, sweeping gesture with his hand at all the land surrounding them.

"This ranch is half yours now," he said. "I'm sure you'll think of something."

"It'll be lonesome here without you," she said wistfully.

29

"You'll survive."

"I'll try, but I'll still miss you."

Butch didn't reply. He studied her a moment, and then he kicked up his horse. The men fell in behind him as they trotted out of headquarters.

Lucy stood on the porch and counted silently. Including Butch, there were twenty-eight riders.

She watched them until they had disappeared over the hill. The men at the barn returned to their chores, and Lucy was left alone.

She walked away from the house a ways, stopped, and studied the landscape in all directions.

"Half mine," she repeated slowly. A few seconds passed, and she added, "For now."

Part 2
"Old Friends"

Chapter eight

A few days later, the town council held an unexpected meeting.

Rondo Landon rarely liked surprises, and he was skeptical when Ross came and told him.

"What's this all about?" He asked as they walked down the street.

"All Fred Stilwell told me is to fetch you," Ross replied. "He said they had something important to discuss."

Rondo grunted, but didn't reply.

Rondo was small and hard bodied, and he was also well known for the ivory-handled Colt that he always displayed on his right hip.

As for Ross, he had a tall and lanky frame, with tanned skin and brown hair. When he spoke he always displayed a rich, Texan drawl.

The meeting was taking place at the jail. This irritated Rondo, because the jail was *his* office, not the town council's.

They passed Rondo's house, and his wife Rachel was sitting out on the front porch.

She had long, brown hair with sandy looking freckles that covered her face. She also had a knowing smile that always made Rondo squirm, and she was giving him that look now.

Despite his foul mood, Rondo couldn't help but smile back.

"Where are you two headed?" She asked.

Rondo gestured at the jail.

"Town council wants to hold a meeting."

"Can I come?"

"Sure," Rondo said, and she smiled and bounded off the porch.

The three town council members were waiting as they entered the jail. There was also another man there, and Rondo frowned irritably when he spotted him.

He was sitting in Rondo's chair, his feet up on his desk.

He had a leathery face with a hard jaw and cold eyes. He was a tall man, and despite the smirk on his face, Rondo could tell that there was no kindness in him.

The mood was somber, and Rondo was suspicious. They'd had meetings before, but not like this.

"What's going on?" He demanded to know.

Fred Stilwell stepped forward. He looked nervous as he cleared his throat.

"Rondo, we consider you to be a good friend. The first thing we want to say is that we really appreciate the job you've done. The way you handled Ike's men was impressive. *Very* impressive."

"Thanks," Rondo said stiffly.

"But," Fred added, "We're extremely disappointed with how you handled the situation with Lee Mattingly."

"What situation?"

The man behind the desk swung his feet off the desk, stood, and walked over.

"Allow me to explain," he said in a hard, curt voice. "I've been asking around, and you did nothing as Lee Mattingly rode into town and murdered Ron Gallegan. And, to make matters worse, afterwards you encouraged them to leave. You should have arrested him and Brian Clark both."

"Do I know you?" Rondo narrowed his eyes.

"My name is Rock. Rock Bullen."

Rondo had heard of him, but he hid his surprise.

"It was self defense," Rondo argued instead.

"That's not for you to decide," Rock replied, and added, "Your job is to arrest them."

"If I want your opinion, I'll ask," Rondo replied curtly. "I know how to do my job."

33

"It's not your job anymore," Rock said smugly, and he turned to Fred. "Ain't that right?"

Fred looked fidgety as Rondo turned toward him.

"Is that true?" He asked.

"I'm sorry, Rondo," Fred said wistfully. "But we've got to let you go. Ron Gallegan was a very important man back east, and everybody knows that you and Lee are friends. It just doesn't look good, especially since you let him escape."

A heavy silence filled the room.

Rondo just stood there with his face pinched in thought. Several tense seconds passed before he looked back at Rock.

"What are you doing here?" He asked.

"I've been hired to bring Lee Mattingly in, dead or alive," Rock announced, and added, "Brian Clark too."

"Who hired you?"

"Wouldn't you like to know?"

"Well, good luck with that," Rondo said flatly.

Rock made a grunting sound. Rondo wasn't sure, but he thought it might have been an attempt at a laugh.

Rondo was furious, but he managed to control his emotions. He nodded slowly as he grasped the situation, and he removed his sheriff's badge that was pinned on his vest.

He started to toss it onto the floor, but decided against it. Instead, he walked over to the desk and put it down gently.

Rondo turned and looked at each member of the town council. His gaze was honest and direct, and each member dropped their eyes.

Next, he looked at Ross. He was just standing there, hands in his pockets, looking thoughtful.

Rondo turned to Rachel and held out his hand.

"Let's go," he said softly.

Rachel forced a smile. She took her husband's hand, and they headed toward the door.

34

"There's one more thing," Fred called out after them, and his voice was hoarse.

"What is it?" Rondo stopped and looked back.

"Your house. We'll need it for the new sheriff."

Rondo nodded curtly.

"We'll be out today."

"I'm sorry, Rondo," Fred said. "I really am."

"Sure."

As they walked out, Rondo heard Fred say, "Ross, we'd like to talk to you."

Chapter nine

Rondo showed no emotion as they packed their belongings. But Rachel was furious, and she let her feelings be known.

"After all you did for this town, and this is how they repay you!" She seethed.

Rondo just shrugged.

"What will we do now?" She asked.

"I'll get another job," Rondo said flatly.

"Doing what?"

"I don't know yet, Rachel."

"My father would hire you back. He'd be glad to."

"I know," Rondo said softly, and added, "We'll see."

"But we'd have no place to live," she continued. "There's only the bunkhouse and the main house."

"Yes, I know that," Rondo said patently. It was silent, and he looked up suddenly. "There is something I've got to do."

"What's that?"

"Lee and Brian," he explained. "They need to know about Rock Bullen."

"Do you know where they went?"

"I have a general idea."

Rachel's face filled with worry.

"You could get into trouble," she objected.

"They're my friends. I'm not sure if you've noticed, but I don't have many."

"Ross is your friend."

Rondo scowled at his wife and grunted in response.

"I know they're your friends, but Lee and Brian also broke the law," she pointed out.

"That's not how I see it."

Rachel frowned. A few minutes passed, and the silence was heavy as they finished packing.

36

"J.T. Tussle told me once if I ever wanted a job, to come see him," Rondo said thoughtfully. "Mebbe after I warn Lee, I'll go talk to him."

Rondo paused and glanced at Rachel.

"I can travel faster alone, so I'll leave you with your parents," he decided.

Rachel didn't like the thought of being left, but she knew that her husband was right.

"When will you leave?" She asked.

"Tomorrow."

"How long will all this take?"

"I'm not sure. A few weeks, give or take."

"That's a long time."

"I'll hurry," Rondo smiled.

"You'd better," she tried to smile back.

They picked up their few belongings and headed toward the door. Rondo walked out briskly, but Rachel paused. She took a slow look at the empty house, and she tried not to cry as she turned and followed after her husband.

Rondo was standing rigid on the porch. Rachel looked up and spotted Ross walking towards them.

He had his hands in his pockets and looked fidgety.

"What are you doing here?" Rondo asked, and he couldn't help but sound bitter.

"Aw, don't be like that, Rondo," Ross said wistfully.

"Are you the new sheriff?"

"They offered me the job."

"And?"

"I told them I would think about it."

"What's there to think about?" Rondo asked sharply. "You wanted to be sheriff. Here's your chance."

"I wouldn't do that to you."

"Did you have anything to do with me being fired?" Rondo asked bluntly.

"Of course not."

37

"Then don't be foolish. Somebody's got to be sheriff. Might as well be you."

"You won't be sore?"

"Not at you."

"I appreciate you saying that. I really do."

Rondo nodded, and Ross looked relieved.

"What are you going to do now?" Ross asked.

"We're still discussing that."

"If there's anything I can do to help-."

"Thanks."

Ross just stood there looking uncomfortable, and a few awkward seconds passed.

"Well, I'll see you around," Ross finally said.

Rondo nodded.

"Sure," he said softly.

Chapter ten

Rondo and Rachel rode up to the Tomlin's headquarters just in time for supper.

It was an impressive layout. The main house was long and big, and the pole corrals were well kept and in good shape, as was the barn and bunkhouse.

Besides Rondo and Rachel, there were four others at supper. Mr. and Mrs. Tomlin, Buster, and the young ranch hand Rory Wheeler.

Craig Tomlin had white hair, and his face was weathered and wrinkled. But his eyes were attentive and sharp, and he never seemed to miss a thing.

He looked thoughtful during supper, and afterwards everyone drifted out onto the front porch. They got comfortable, and Mr. Tomlin looked over at Rondo.

"Well, what happened?"

"How'd you know something was wrong?" Rondo was surprised.

"Only by the strained look on your faces," Mr. Tomlin explained.

Rondo grinned sheepishly, but his expression turned dark as he explained all that had happened.

"I hate to leave Rachel here," he finished, "but it'll only take me a few weeks to warn Lee and then go see Tussle."

Mr. Tomlin nodded as he thought it over.

"We'll help any way we can," he said, and added bitterly, "I'll also be talking to the town council about this. What a foolish bunch, to fire the best sheriff Empty-lake ever had."

"Don't cause any trouble on my account," Rondo looked worried.

Mr. Tomlin grunted in response and stood.

"If you're leaving at sun up, we'd best get to bed," he suggested.

39

"Yes, sir," Rondo smiled.

***

Sun up came early.

While Rondo saddled his horse, Mrs. Tomlin made breakfast. It was a quick meal, and afterwards everybody gathered in front of the house.

Rondo said goodbye to everyone, and afterwards they all backed off and left him and Rachel alone.

Rachel smiled warmly at Rondo, and he got that weak feeling in his knees again.

"Well, you go do what you have to do," she said.

"I will."

"Just come back to me."

"I plan to," Rondo promised.

He kissed her gently, climbed on his horse, and rode out.

***

Rondo trotted back to town.

He needed supplies, so he pulled up at the general store. He bought canned goods and coffee and packed them in his saddlebags.

He was almost done when he spotted April Gibson. She was hurrying down the street toward him, and she looked tense and anxious,

April worked at The Palace Hotel. She was a tall, graceful looking woman with a wisp of natural gray hair here and there.

She had strong feelings for Lee Mattingly, and almost everybody in town knew it.

"I heard what happened," she said as she walked up. "I'm so sorry for you and Rachel."

"Don't be," Rondo replied. "We'll be all right."

"You're leaving town," she observed.

40

"Yes, I've got some things to tend to."

"Is Rachel going with you?"

"Not this time."

"I see," April nodded. She hesitated, and then blurted, "Will you see Lee?"

Rondo was surprised by the question. He studied her a moment and nodded.

"It's a strong possibility."

"When you do, could you give him a message?"

"I can do that."

"Tell him-," she paused, and a wistful look crossed her face. "Tell him there's a little girl named June that prays every night for Mister Lee to come back. Would you please tell him that?"

Rondo's face turned soft.

"Sure. I'll tell him," he promised.

"Thank you," April said, and added, "Good luck."

"Thank you, ma'am."

April nodded. She looked like she wanted to say something else, but instead she turned abruptly and hurried down the street.

Rondo watched her leave, and then he stepped into the saddle and kicked up his horse.

As he rode out of town, Rock Bullen watched curiously from the shadows beside the hotel.

Chapter eleven

Rondo knew the general direction Lee and Brian had gone. He rode out of town a few miles, and then he rode in a big semi-circle, looking for tracks.

He finally found some sign, but following the trail was painfully slow.

Now and then he would see a faded hoof print, but mostly he followed them through horse droppings and the signs of old campfires.

Three days out, he got the distinct feeling that he was being followed. He did his best to cover his tracks, and when he was on high ground he would watch his back trail for several hours at a time.

He never saw anything. But still, no matter how careful he was, he just couldn't shake the feeling.

Because of this, at nighttime he didn't risk the light of a campfire. Instead, his camps were dark, and he sipped water from his canteen while he ate his canned goods.

The landscape started to change a few days later. The ground got rougher, and there were steep hills, more rocks, and a few canyons. There were also some small ponds that were spring filled spread about.

Rondo smiled as he remembered back. Ben Kinrich often liked to hide out in these same canyons after pulling a job.

There was a particular canyon that Rondo remembered being ahead, and Lee and Brian's trail led to the opening. It was a deep descend to the bottom, and the walls were mostly rock.

The trail split at the base of the canyon.

Rondo dismounted and studied the ground, but there were no markings to suggest which way they had gone.

As he squatted there, he suddenly heard a chipping sound. It was faint, but Rondo could still tell that it was a horse traveling on the rocks behind him.

His horse heard it too, and his head came up sharply.

"Easy, Desperate," Rondo spoke softly.

He frowned thoughtfully as he studied the terrain.

The trail to the west went towards higher ground, and he nodded as he came to a decision.

He turned towards his horse. He checked his rifle and Colt, and then he climbed into the saddle and nudged Desperate forward.

Chapter twelve

Lee Mattingly held a thick cigar in one hand, and in the other he held a long, slender cedar limb. All the bark and twigs had been carefully whittled off, and the end result was a smooth fishing pole.

A fishing line made from horsehair and rawhide had been tied to the end, and a crudely built hook was at the end of the line, baited down with worms.

Lee was in his mid-thirties. He had a gentleman-like way about him, and he had a different set of ethics than most outlaws. He was soft spoken, and was loyal to those that he considered friends.

Brian Clark sat beside Lee, and they were both resting under the shade of a tall tree. They watched Lee's fishing line as it playfully swayed in the water.

Brian was in his mid-fifties. He was a grizzled veteran, and he was wanted in nearly every territory or state there was.

Like Lee, Brian also had a gentle-like way about him. He was always careful; he never took any chances unless he had to.

"Fishing is a skill," Lee was saying as he took a puff on his cigar. "You have to know how to find the fish, how to approach them, and what bait to use."

"You sound like an expert, but your results suggest otherwise," Brian replied matter-of-factly. "We've been here for days, but so far all you've snagged is a branch."

"It takes time," Lee frowned.

"You've proved that."

"If we had more horses I could have made two lines," Lee commented.

"I don't mind. It's more fun watching you."

Lee grunted, and it fell silent.

44

A few minutes passed. Lee took in a deep breath, and he looked wistful as he exhaled.

Brian looked sideways and studied his friend with a thoughtful look.

"Miss them, don't you?"

"Miss who?" Lee looked startled.

"You know who," Brian shot Lee a dark look. "April and June."

Lee started to deny it, but then he stopped. He sighed and nodded miserably.

"I'd be a fool if I didn't," he admitted softly.

"We should have brought them with us."

"We've already discussed this," Lee said irritably. "We're wanted outlaws, remember?"

"But Yancy promised us a pardon."

"Yes, but that was before I killed that politician."

"It was self defense," Brian argued, and added, "Rondo saw it. He'll testify."

Lee nodded slowly as he thought on that.

"After we visit Jessica, perhaps we should ride into Midway and explain what happened to Yancy," Lee figured. "Mebbe he and Judge Parker can do something."

"After all we did for them, I reckon they owe us," Brian agreed, and then he asked, "Speaking of Jessica, don't you think it's time we went and saw her?"

"I reckon it is," Lee looked hesitant, and he admitted, "Tell you the truth, I've been dragging my feet on purpose. I'm not all that anxious for another confrontation with her. Her last words stung me like a whip."

"But this time we have good news," Brian reminded. "We got her hotel back."

"I don't think that'll matter much. She hates me."

"Hate might be too strong a word. Dislike sounds better."

"No, I think hate is the perfect word."

"April and June don't hate you."

45

"You just *have* to keep reminding me of that," Lee scowled.

"I don't want you to forget about them," Brian said truthfully.

"I won't. Especially with you around."

"Good," Brian looked pleased, and he added, "I liked April and June."

"Why don't you marry her then?"

"She loves you."

Lee was startled, and he frowned to cover it.

"You're talking too much," he said roughly. "Scaring the fish away."

"You're talking just as much as I am."

Lee glared at Brian. He started to respond, but his fishing pole danced in his hand before he could. He grunted in surprise, and his cigar dropped to the ground as he grabbed the limb with both hands.

"I've got one!" He exclaimed.

"Looks like a fighter too!" Brian added enthusiastically.

They jumped to their feet, and Lee instinctively yanked back on the cedar limb.

"Easy now, or you'll lose him!" Brian instructed.

"I know what I'm doing!" Lee yelled harshly.

He stepped into the water, all the while tugging on his cedar limb. He kept walking forward, and before he knew it he was waist deep.

Brian laughed and followed after him.

"He's a big one!" Lee exclaimed.

He yanked back sharply. A loud crack sounded out, and the cedar limb snapped. They were both helpless as the broken limb hit the water.

"I told you to cut a green limb," Brian chided. "It wouldn't have broken so easy."

Lee didn't reply as Brian waded up beside him, and they watched somberly as their fishing line disappeared.

Several seconds passed, and they suddenly realized that they were soaking wet.

They looked at each other. Brian chuckled, and then they both laughed.

It felt good to ease their tension. However, their jovial mood changed abruptly when they turned around.

There was a man on a horse beside the bank, and he had a cruel snarl on his face. His rifle was laid over his saddle in front of him, and it was pointed straight at them.

Chapter thirteen

"Move and I'll kill you," the man warned them in a rough, curt voice.

"Take it easy. We ain't looking for trouble," Brian spoke up, and asked, "Who are you? Want do you want?"

"The name's Rock Bullen," he announced. "I'm hunting two outlaws."

Brian glanced at Lee and looked back at Rock.

"No outlaws around here," he said.

"Sure," Rock laughed, but not humorously.

Lee stood perfectly still in the water. An irritated feeling was coming over him, and he scowled, thrust out his jaw, and glared at Rock.

"Who are these outlaws you're looking for?" He demanded to know.

"Lee Mattingly is one of them," Rock replied, unmoved by Lee's stare. "You heard of him?"

"Who hasn't?" Lee smiled tightly. "A real ladies man. Supposed to be mighty handsome. Good with a gun too."

Rock grunted and asked, "How 'bout Brian Clark? You heard of him too?"

"Sure. He's the ugly one."

Brian scowled, but Lee's face remained the same.

Rock pulled the hammer back on his rifle, and it made a soft click.

"You heard of me?" Rock asked softly.

"Some," Lee said.

"You heard I don't take prisoners?"

"I've heard that, yes. You must not like conversation."

"That is correct," Rock's eyes glowed in triumph, and he raised his rifle to his shoulder.

"You're making a mistake," Lee said.

"You ain't Lee and Brian?"

48

Lee wasn't in the mood to lie. He took in a deep breath, narrowed his eyes, and exhaled.

"We're them," he said flatly.

"Thought so."

"I don't reckon it would do us any good to say that we're innocent."

"That's right. It wouldn't."

"But we are innocent."

"That ain't my problem," Rock said, and without another word he took aim.

"Run for it!" Lee shouted at Brian, and they lunged through the water.

A rifle shot sounded out, and Lee instinctively fell backwards. He thought he'd been shot, but then he realized that he hadn't.

There was a whining sound as a bullet ricocheted, and Rock's horse jumped forward. Three more rifle shots bellowed out, and the bullets slammed into the rock surface around Rock's horse.

The horse was spooked, and Rock lowered his rifle as he fought to keep him under control. Meanwhile, Lee and Brian reached the bank.

More bullets came whining down, and Rock cursed. He slammed his spurs into the side of his horse, and the terrified animal took out in a dead run.

Lee and Brian grabbed their rifles and fired at the retreating bounty hunter. But he was moving too fast, and their hasty shots missed.

"You hit?" Brian gasped as they hunkered down behind the tree.

"Don't think so," Lee looked himself over to be sure. "You?"

"Nope. Whoever's shooting must not be shooting at us."

"I'm glad he jumped in, but whoever's up there is a terrible shot," Lee muttered as he peered upwards. "He completely missed Rock."

49

"Looked to me like he done it on purpose," Brian said. "Probably wanted to just scare him off."

Lee snorted his displeasure. He started to respond, but suddenly he grunted in surprise and jolted forward.

"What's the matter?" Brian asked, worried.

A sheepish look crossed Lee's face.

"My cigar," he explained. "I was squatting on it."

"You and your cigars," Brian muttered. It was silent, and then he scowled, looked at Lee, and asked, "The ugly one?"

"Sorry 'bout that. I was under pressure."

"Sure you was."

Chapter fourteen

Lee and Brian were wet and irritable. They stayed hunkered down behind the tree, holding their rifles as they inspected the surrounding area.

They finally heard the sound of a horse as it came down the trail.

There was no need to say anything. Lee glanced at Brian, and he nodded back.

They pulled back the hammers on their rifles and waited.

A rider appeared a few seconds later. Lee took aim, but he halted when he recognized him.

"It's Rondo," he grunted in surprise.

"Sure is," Brian replied.

Lee cleared his throat and called out, "Rondo! It's us, Lee and Brian."

They stepped out into the open. Rondo spotted them, and he grinned as he trotted up.

"Hello, Lee," he drawled, and he nodded at Brian. "Good to see you, Brian."

"Likewise," Brian said.

It was silent as they studied each other, and then Lee asked, "What are you doing out here, Rondo?"

"I came to warn you about Rock."

"You're a little late, ain't you?"

"I didn't think I was."

"He was about to kill us," Lee scowled.

"I noticed that."

"And then you missed him," Lee frowned his disapproval.

An innocent look crossed Rondo's face.

"It happens."

"Not to you, it doesn't," Lee grumbled, and asked, "Why didn't you kill him?"

"You wanted me to shoot him in the back?" Rondo raised an eyebrow.

"Yes," Lee declared matter-of-factly. "When a man's trying to kill me, I'm real quick to give him the same treatment."

"But he wasn't trying to kill me," Rondo pointed out.

"He will be next time," Lee replied sourly, and added, "And there will be a next time. He's not the sort that gives up."

"Perhaps."

"You and your silly rules," Lee sighed, and then he changed the subject. "So, you rode all the way out here just to warn us?"

"Partly," Rondo replied. "I'm also headed for Midway."

"On law business?"

"I'm not the sheriff. Not anymore."

"What?" Lee and Brian were startled.

A dark look crossed Rondo's face as he explained.

"There's gratitude for you," Lee mumbled when Rondo had finished.

"I'm not complaining," Rondo shrugged. "I've always enjoyed punching cows. It's more peaceful."

"I reckon it is," Lee agreed. He thought the situation over and added, "We're headed for Midway too. You want to ride with us?"

"Sounds good."

"Course, with Rock being out there, it might be a little dangerous riding with us," Lee warned.

"Naw," Rondo grinned. "We won't be *in* danger. We *are* the danger."

"If you're talking about the entire Landon clan, then I agree."

"How's that?" Rondo looked confused.

"Yancy's been after me for years, Cooper shot me a while back, and now you lead a bounty hunter straight to my camp."

52

"Coop *shot* you?"

"He sure did," Lee patted his shoulder.

Rondo frowned as he thought on that.

"Coop usually doesn't shoot anybody without good reason."

Lee was silent, so Brian cleared his throat.

"Lee and Yancy were about to shoot each other," he explained.

"What for?"

"It doesn't matter now," Lee spoke back up, and added, "We have an arrangement now."

"I hope it's a peaceful arrangement."

"We've held up our end. It's up to Yancy now."

"He'll come through," Rondo vowed.

"We'll see," Lee said, and he turned towards their camp. "I reckon we should ride a few miles before dark. Probably not safe to camp here tonight."

Rondo nodded, and as they packed up camp he looked around.

He was startled when he noticed their horses. Instead of having long tails, all three had short stumps.

"What happened to your horses' tails?" He asked.

Lee didn't say anything, so Brain explained.

"Lee wanted to go fishing," he said, "and we didn't have a fishing line."

"I see," Rondo said, and his eyes lit up in anticipation. "Catch anything for supper?"

"Nope."

"Oh."

Chapter fifteen

Rock Bullen was furious, and mostly at himself.

He was a careful and cunning man who liked to be in control of his surroundings. He was the one who usually ambushed others.

But this time he had been the prey. If the shooter had wanted him dead, he would be.

It was a difficult thing to swallow as he rode out of the canyon and trotted west.

He suddenly became aware of the wetness on his leg. He looked down and discovered that his canteen had a huge gaping hole.

He scowled. All the water was gone, and that meant no coffee tonight.

Rock wanted to put some distance between him and the canyon before he stopped. He trotted briskly, and when it got dark he just kept going. The moon was mostly full, and he could see the ground just fine.

He thought his current situation over as he rode.

Lee and Brian were riding north. There was only one major town in that direction, and that was Midway.

It would be dangerous to follow. They were expecting him now, and an ambush was likely. There was also the shooter from the ridge to consider.

Rock finally decided to ride to Midway and wait for them there. He would also take another route to avoid ambush.

Satisfied, Rock decided to stop for the night.

He found a decent spot, and he was just about to dismount when he spotted a glow of a campfire in the distance.

He frowned thoughtfully as he wondered who it might be.

It would be safer to ride around, but the thought of getting a cup of coffee changed his mind.

He checked his Colt and kicked up his horse.

As he rode closer he could hear occasional laughter. He could also make out several men gathered around the fire, plus a few lookouts.

One of the lookouts heard him coming, and Rock heard the click of a rifle hammer.

"Who's out there?" The lookout called out.

"Hold your fire," Rock replied. "I'm looking for a cup of coffee, is all."

"Ride on in, but take it easy," the lookout cautioned.

"Take it easy yourself," Rock said, and he walked his horse forward.

Everybody around the fire had stood, and most held their rifles. Rock looked them over, and he grunted when he recognized the leader.

It was Butch Nelson and his men.

If Butch was surprised, he didn't show it. Instead, he narrowed his eyes as he studied him.

"What are you doing here?"

"I told you," Rock replied. "I'm looking for a cup of coffee."

"Help yourself," Butch nodded at the coffee pot.

Rock nodded. He dismounted, tied his horse to a nearby bush, dug his cup out of his saddlebags, and walked over to the fire.

"Preciate it," he said as he squatted by the coals.

Butch watched as he poured a cup of steaming coffee. He took a swig, sighed in contentment, and wiped his mouth with his sleeve.

"Good coffee," he said.

"Traveling kind of late, ain't you?" Butch changed the subject.

"You could say that."

"What about Lee and Brian? Did you get them?"

Rock ignored the questions as he took another swig. Several seconds passed, and he looked over at Butch. Both were motionless as they stared at each other.

"I have a job to do," he said softly.

"I know. I'm the one who hired you."

"But I'll do it my own way, in my own time."

"I ain't in a particular hurry," Butch shrugged, and added, "Just as long as they don't die of old age."

Rock grunted and changed the subject.

"Where you headed?" He asked.

"Midway."

"What for?"

"Business."

"What sort of business?"

A suspicious look crossed Butch's face.

"Why do you care?"

"Just curious."

It was silent as Butch thought on that, and then he shrugged.

"If you must know, we're going to raid J.T. Tussle's ranch."

Rock was surprised. He finished his coffee and rose to his feet.

"Tussle can be a handful," he warned.

"I know that."

"How are you going to go about it?"

"Perfectly, I hope."

Rock grunted his response. He studied Butch a moment more and cleared his throat.

"Things like that take careful planning," he said, and added, "I could help if you wanted. I have experience in such matters."

Butch gave him a hard, calculating look.

"What about Lee and Brian?"

"They're headed toward Midway."

"You're sure?"

"Pretty much."

Butch scratched his stubbled jaw in thought.

"You've done this sorta work before?"

"Some."

"I thought you were a bounty hunter."

"I haven't always been."

"Well, I ain't desperate, but I reckon I can use all the help I can muster going against Tussle."

"I'd say so."

"Especially fellas with experience."

"That would be me."

"All right. You can ride with us," Butch decided, and asked, "Now, what's this careful planning you was talking about?"

Rock shook his head.

"Before we get into that, we need to agree on the price."

Butch scowled at him.

"How much you want?"

"Double wages will do. For now."

"For now?"

"I like to keep my options open. You never know when conditions might change."

Butch grunted. It was silent for a moment, and he sighed and nodded.

"Fine," he muttered. "Double wages."

Rock smiled. He refilled his coffee cup, got comfortable by the fire, and looked up at Butch.

"When we get there, I'd split your forces," he announced. "Except for one. You'll need somebody to stay with the mules and extra horses."

"You want us to split up?" Butch narrowed his eyes. "Why?"

"They'll probably be holding the herd close to headquarters," Rock figured.

"I'd say so."

"It'd be best if we attacked the herd and headquarters all at once," Rock explained. "Take everybody by one, big surprise."

Butch liked that, and he nodded slowly.

"Go on," he said.

Rock grinned wolfishly and cleared his throat.

Chapter sixteen

"That's a fine looking packhorse," Rondo commented as they made their way out of the canyon.

Lee was in front, and he led the packhorse. Rondo was next, and Brian brought up the rear.

"He no look so good," Brian said in a thick, Spanish accent.

"How's that?" Rondo asked, confused.

"He's the gentlest, best handling, smoothest horse you ever rode," Brian said, and added, "But he's also almost completely blind. We call him No-see-ums."

"That's a shame," Rondo said as he admired the animal.

"Sure is."

They rode a while in silence.

Then Rondo said, "I almost forgot. I got a message to deliver."

"From who?" Lee turned in the saddle and looked back.

"April."

The mere mention of her name sent trills of excitement through Lee. He tried to hide it by frowning and looking unconcerned.

"Oh? What did she say?"

Rondo told him, and Lee felt a pinch in his stomach. He was suddenly irritable, and he turned back around in the saddle so the others couldn't see his face.

"I wonder why she'd say that?" He asked nonchalantly.

Rondo frowned.

"You don't know?"

"Know what?"

"April has strong feelings for you. She's been miserable since you left."

"What about Jeremiah Wisdom?" There was bitterness in Lee's voice.

"What about him?"

59

"Don't they have feelings for each other?"

"He might, but she doesn't. Everybody in town knows who she has feelings for, except for mebbe you."

It was silent, and then Lee declared, "Well, she'll just have to get over it."

"Why?" Rondo asked, perplexed.

"Because she's a real lady, and I'm an outlaw and a killer."

"I used to be those things too," Rondo reminded, and added, "I changed."

"I tried, but it didn't work."

Rondo wanted to change his mind, but he could tell that Lee wasn't in the mood. So, Rondo decided to change the subject.

"Well, it'll take us a few weeks to reach Midway," he said.

"And we'll have to keep watch every night too," Lee added sourly.

"Pretty sure we can handle it," Rondo smiled tightly.

Lee muttered a reply, and it fell silent.

A few minutes passed, and Brian suddenly chuckled.

"What are you snickering about?" Lee looked back at Brian and scowled.

"It just occurred to me that we're all that's left of Kinrich's old outfit," Brian explained. "Together one last time."

"Who says it'll be the last time?" Rondo asked.

"It might be if Rock catches us," Lee retorted.

Rondo sighed and shot his friend a dark look.

"Are you going to stay in a bad mood the entire trip?"

"Probably."

You must really miss April, Rondo thought, and he smiled as he wondered how long it would take for Lee to give in.

Part Three
"The Attack"
A few weeks later

Chapter seventeen

Today was J.T. Tussle's birthday. Unawares to him, his niece Jessica had planned a celebration supper.

It would be a small gathering. The only folks invited besides the ranch foreman were the Landons.

Yancy and Cooper trotted their horses across Tussle's range towards headquarters. Cooper's wife Josie and their adopted son Wyatt trailed along behind them.

Yancy was a very somber man. He never talked unless he had to, and when he did it was always clear, certain, and to the point. He was also painfully honest, no matter the cost.

He was also well respected for his skills with his Colt six-shooter. However, Cooper was just as dangerous.

Tall and wide shouldered, Cooper wasn't nearly as good with a Colt. Instead, his specialty was with his Henry rifle. He was real accurate with it, and mighty quick too. He had a special way of swinging it up, and it was almost as fast as Yancy's draw.

Cooper was also a very good tracker.

Both brothers were newly appointed Texas Rangers, and their first assignment was to crush the corrupt empire that Ike Nash had created. Ike was now dead, thanks to Lee Mattingly, but there was still work to do.

As for Josie, she had a sharp, young-looking face with long, brown hair. And, underneath her appearance was an undeniable strength.

Wyatt was tall and thin. His face was covered with sandy looking freckles, and he had dark hair.

Yancy and Cooper had recently rescued Wyatt from the Apaches. He had nowhere to go, so Cooper and Josie took him in.

Despite Josie's efforts, he still wouldn't talk much. Josie and Cooper were worried about that, but Yancy didn't mind so much.

Yancy's freshly shaved face itched as they neared headquarters. He scratched his neck and shifted nervously in the saddle.

Cooper glanced sideways at his younger brother and raised an eyebrow.

"What's the matter?"

"Oh, nothing much."

"Doesn't look like nothing. Your face is red as a tomato."

Yancy didn't reply, and Cooper waited patiently. A few seconds passed, and Yancy took in a deep breath and sighed.

"If you must know, I'm trying to think of something to say."

"To Jessica?"

Yancy nodded.

"This is the third time you've had supper with her," Cooper pointed out, and asked, "You still can't carry on a decent conversation with her?"

Yancy nodded, more solemnly this time.

"Try not to be a blabber mouth," Cooper encouraged.

Yancy shot Cooper a dark look, and it was silent as he searched for the right words.

"Whenever I'm around her, I just run out of things to say," he finally admitted. "Mostly, we just sit there."

"That sounds painful."

"It is."

"When you do talk, what do you talk about?"

"Mostly about the weather," he replied, and his face lightened as a thought occurred to him. "I did tell her about me killing Rocca. I think she liked that."

Cooper groaned and shook his head.

"This is worse than I thought."

63

"How's that?" Yancy looked offended.

"Women don't care about the weather or killing people," Cooper explained patently. "You need to compliment her. Tell her she looks nice. She'd like that."

Yancy nodded as he made a mental note.

"Anything else?"

"I ain't the one courting her."

Yancy frowned and looked frustrated.

"She doesn't talk much either," he complained.

"That's probably 'cause she's just as nervous as you."

"Mebbe it's hopeless," Yancy sounded tired.

"Not quite, but it's close."

"You know who Jessica reminds me of?" Yancy asked suddenly.

"Who?" Cooper looked curious.

"Me."

Cooper glanced sideways and studied Yancy thoughtfully.

"Yes," Cooper wisecracked. "The physical resemblance is quite striking."

"That's not what I meant," Yancy scowled. "We both seem to struggle with the same things."

Cooper grinned, and his white teeth shone at his brother.

"Just relax," he instructed. "Try to have fun."

"Fun?"

"Yes, fun. I'm sure you've seen others experiencing it."

Yancy scowled again, and Cooper chuckled as they trotted on.

64

Chapter eighteen

The headquarters at Tussle's ranch was impressive.

The main house was huge, multi-roomed, and had numerous windows that opened up to the spacious front porch.

Across from the main house was the cookhouse and a large bunkhouse, and beyond that was a barn, a set of corrals, a saddle house, and some storage sheds.

It was an eventful time. The cattle drive to Kansas was fast approaching, and the ranch hands were busy getting prepared.

All of Tussle's stock had already been gathered. The yearlings that were to be sold had been sorted out, and the mother cows had been scattered back over the range. The herd of yearlings was being held beside a spring about a mile from headquarters.

Tussle had hired a few extra hands for the drive, and they were staying out with the herd. Their job was to keep the herd together, and every day they would move the herd so they could graze.

Meanwhile, the remuda had also been gathered, and the horses were being held in a huge pen, called a dry lot, at headquarters.

Most of the horses hadn't been ridden in months, and a half dozen cowpunchers were topping off the horses as the Landons rode in.

There were some impressive bronc rides going on, and the Landons pulled up at the corrals and watched.

"I never could ride a bucking horse," Yancy commented.

"Nor a bucking mule," Cooper reminded with a wry smile.

"Jug-head bucked you off too," Yancy frowned.

"He did," Cooper admitted.

65

"I'd sell that mule, if'n I was you," Yancy said as they kicked up their horses and headed for the main house.

"I have, but he keeps coming back."

Yancy snorted. They dismounted, tied their horses to the hitching rail, and stepped up onto the front porch.

Cooper knocked, and the sound carried loudly. They heard footsteps, and the door opened.

Tussle stood there, and he frowned curiously.

"What are you doing here?"

Yancy was silent, so Cooper smiled and cleared his throat.

"We were invited," he explained. "Something about a birthday."

"I declare," Tussle scowled. "Nobody tells me anything around here anymore."

He mumbled some more as he stepped back and allowed them in.

Tussle was an ex rebel, and proud of it. He respected the Landons, but he also never forgot that they had fought on different sides.

He was a tall man with a wide frame. He had a weathered face that was trenched with deep lines, and those lines changed shape when he smiled or frowned.

"You probably want to see Jessica," he told Yancy, and he nodded towards the kitchen. "She's back there."

"Thanks," Yancy said stiffly.

Everyone else went into the dining room while Yancy breathed deeply and walked towards the back.

He spotted Jessica in the kitchen, and he stopped in the dark hallway and watched her for a moment.

Jessica was in her early twenties. She had a good figure, long blond hair, and light blue eyes. And, as Yancy had already found out, she also had a very feisty side.

At the moment, her face was flushed and hot as she worked over the stove.

66

She finally turned and spotted him. Their eyes met, and several seconds passed.

"Hello," she finally said.

"Jessica," Yancy said stiffly. "Looks good."

"Me, or the meal?" Jessica said coyly, and Yancy's heart thumped.

"Both," Yancy managed.

Jessica smiled, pleased. They looked at each other some more, and then she asked, "Coffee?"

"Sure."

She poured him a cup, and she also handed him the sugar bowl. He put three spoonfuls in, stirred, and took a swig.

The coffee had a burnt taste.

Yancy forced himself to swallow, and he coughed to cover his dislike.

"Do you like it?" Jessica asked hopefully.

Yancy was not one to lie, and several seconds passed as he thought on how to reply.

"No," he finally said. "But, I sure like your sugar."

Chapter nineteen

Supper was pleasant.

Yancy, Josie, and Jessica made small talk. Tussle mostly just sat there, irritated because everybody knew it was his birthday. James Watts, the ranch foreman, didn't talk much either, nor did Wyatt. As for Cooper, he only talked whenever the conversation started to die.

After supper, Jessica stood and got everyone's attention.

"My Uncle is not keen on birthdays," she said, and added," But, I still got him a present."

Tussle scowled as she hurried from the room. She returned moments later, carrying a fancy looking rifle.

"You said you wanted one of those new Winchester '73 rifles, so I got you one," Jessica announced.

Tussle was obviously surprised and humbled.

"You shouldn't have," he chided softly.

"I can afford it," Jessica smiled. She handed him the rifle, gave him a hug, and said, "Happy birthday."

Tussle was embarrassed by all the attention, and he nodded meekly.

"That's a handsome looking rifle," Cooper spoke up.

"It is," Tussle agreed.

He offered it to Cooper, and his eyes lit up in admiration as he handled it.

The Winchester had an oil-finished walnut stock, a blued steel crescent butt plate, and a twenty-inch round barrel.

"It's a mite longer than my Henry," Cooper observed.

"I hear they shoot farther too," Tussle added.

Cooper nodded and turned towards Yancy.

"Want to look at it?" He offered.

Yancy shook his head, and Cooper suddenly noticed that his younger brother looked slightly irritated.

68

"No thanks," Yancy said, and added, "Think I'll get some fresh air."

He grabbed his hat and walked out abruptly.

Cooper frowned curiously and glanced at Jessica.

She was just standing there beside the table, and she looked just as confused as he was.

She recovered quickly. She stacked several dishes and picked them up.

"Well, the dishes need washing," she said.

"I'll help," Josie offered, and she started clearing the table.

Jessica nodded. She turned to leave, but something caught her eye. She walked over to the window and looked out.

"Riders are coming," she announced.

"How many?" Tussle asked.

"Ten, I think."

Tussle grunted in approval and turned to his foreman.

"Have a talk with them, James. If you like the looks of them, put them on. We could use some more help for the drive."

"Yes, sir," James replied.

Tussle and James talked some more about the upcoming cattle drive while Jessica and Josie finished clearing the table.

Cooper gave the rifle back to Tussle. He smiled at Wyatt and went outside.

He found Yancy sitting in a chair on the porch, looking sulky.

"What's the matter with you?" Cooper scowled.

"That rifle," Yancy muttered.

"What about it?"

"You heard her. She just went out and bought it. Probably didn't even ask how much it cost."

"So?"

"I can barely afford to buy a sack of sugar each month."

"What's that got to do with anything?" Cooper asked, confused.

"I can't support her," Yancy said glumly, and added, "Least not the way she's used to living. She lives in a big, fancy house. Anything she wants, she gets. She doesn't need me."

Cooper sighed.

"We've already discussed this," he said patently. "Money ain't everything. In fact, I've heard too much wealth can bring misery and unhappiness."

"Mebbe so, but I wouldn't mind just a *little* unhappiness in my life."

"There are more important things you can offer her."

"Such as?"

"Companionship for one thing," Cooper said, and added, "She's in the kitchen. I want you to go in there and tell her you're sorry."

"Sorry for what?"

"Doesn't matter. Just tell her you're sorry, and then tell her how you feel."

Yancy didn't like the idea, and he scowled.

"If you don't do this, then I'm through helping you," Cooper warned.

It fell silent as Yancy thought on it, and he nodded slowly.

"All right," he decided. "I'll talk to her."

"It's about time," Cooper declared.

Yancy stood, adjusted his gun belt, and walked back inside.

Cooper chuckled softly and shook his head as he lingered on the porch.

He watched the men at the corrals as they saddled another bronc, and then he glanced at the oncoming riders.

They were in a long, single line, and they had slowed their horses to a walk. The sun was setting directly behind them, and that made it hard to make out much.

70

Cooper heard a noise at the door, and he turned as James walked out. He was trimming a cigar, and after he lit it he glanced at Cooper and grinned.

"They ain't in any hurry," he nodded at the riders.

"Don't appear to be," Cooper agreed.

"Slow as they're riding, it'll be dark before they get here."

"Almost," Cooper smiled.

"Tussle wants to see you," James said. "Something to do with Wyatt."

Cooper nodded. He glanced at the riders once more and walked inside.

Chapter twenty

Yancy paused in the doorway of the kitchen.

Jessica and Josie had their backs to him as they washed the dishes in a washtub. He cleared his throat, and they turned around and spotted him.

A stubborn look crossed Jessica's face.

"Yes?"

"Wanted to say thanks," he said stiffly.

"For what?"

"Supper."

"You're quite welcome."

Yancy nodded hesitantly. A few seconds passed, and the silence was awkward.

Josie glanced at Jessica. She smiled knowingly, and without a word she eased by Yancy and left the room.

Jessica looked at Yancy and crossed her arms. It was a direct look, and Yancy felt his face turning red.

"I'm sorry about earlier," he said. "I get grumpy sometimes."

"Did I say something wrong?"

"No, course not."

"Then what was it? Please tell me. I'd like to know."

Yancy stood there and squirmed as he thought on it.

"I've already made a fool of myself tonight," he finally said. "We should discuss this another time."

"Will there be another time?"

"I hope so."

"I'm looking forward to it," Jessica said earnestly.

"Me too."

"You know, we all do foolish things," Jessica said as she dried her hands on a dishrag.

"I bet you haven't."

Jessica laughed.

72

"I was foolish enough to put all the money from my father's plantation in a carpetbag and get on a stagecoach. You know what happened after that."

"You couldn't help that."

"No, but I shouldn't have attempted to transport all that money on a stagecoach," Jessica's eyes twinkled, but then her face got dark as a thought occurred to her. "And you don't even know the latest foolish thing I've done."

"Oh?"

Jessica hesitated, but then decided to explain.

"I got involved in an ill advised business deal and lost nearly everything."

Yancy was startled.

"You lost all that money?"

"Almost. I still have a little, but not much. Please don't tell my Uncle."

Yancy tried to hide his pleased look.

"I won't tell," he promised, and added, "I'm sure it wasn't all your fault."

"It wasn't," an irritated look crossed her face. "Lee Mattingly had a lot to do with it."

"Lee Mattingly!" Yancy's face darkened. "How is he involved?"

"It's a long story."

"I'd sure like to hear it."

"Maybe some other time," Jessica said, and her face suddenly lit up. "Right now, I'd like to discuss something else."

"Like what?"

"Us," Jessica smiled.

Chapter twenty-one

Josie returned from the kitchen as Cooper stepped into the dining room.

Tussle was seated across from Wyatt. They were playing a game of chess, and they were both tense as they studied the board.

Although he would never admit it, Tussle had grown quite fond of Wyatt. He had given him a summer job, and Wyatt did odd jobs around headquarters. He still lived with Cooper and Josie, but he rode out to the ranch every chance he had.

"You wanted to see me?" Cooper asked.

"I did," Tussle nodded.

They halted their game. Tussle stood, walked over to the window, and looked out.

"How old is Wyatt?" He asked.

Josie and Cooper glanced at each other.

"Thirteen, we think," he said.

Tussle grunted his approval and turned from the window.

"I went on my first cattle drive when I was eleven," he declared.

Cooper and Josie didn't know what to say to that, so they just nodded.

"It was a good experience for me," Tussle continued. "I left a boy, but came back a man."

"At eleven years of age?" Cooper narrowed his eyes.

"You know what I mean," Tussle scowled.

"Actually, I'm not sure I do."

"I'd like for Wyatt to go along on the cattle drive," Tussle announced.

Wyatt looked up sharply. He didn't say anything, but his face was flushed with excitement. He looked at Cooper and held his breath as he waited for an answer.

74

Cooper frowned thoughtfully and looked at Josie. As usual, her face showed no expression.

"I don't know, Tussle," Cooper reasoned. "It might be too soon."

"You know I'd look after him," Tussle reassured, and added, "I think it'd be good for him."

"Yes," Josie spoke softly, and Cooper almost jumped in surprise.

"Are you sure?" He looked at her.

"It is time," Josie nodded. "Let him go."

Cooper glanced at Wyatt. He already knew the answer, but he asked it anyway.

"Is this what you want, Wyatt?"

Wyatt's eyes shone with eagerness as he nodded.

"All right then," Cooper looked back at Tussle. "It's settled."

"Good!" Tussle looked pleased, and Wyatt grinned.

Chapter twenty-two

Butch Nelson walked his horse towards Tussle's ranch headquarters.

His rifle was loaded and ready in his scabbard, as was the Colt on his hip. He felt calm and steady.

Nine of his men followed behind him in single file. Nobody talked, and the mood was somber.

Except for Sim, the rest of the men were with Rock. They were well hidden in some nearby trees, waiting to ambush the herd.

Sim had been selected to stay with the mules and extra horses. He was several miles to the north, staying at their camp.

The sun was just setting as they reached the corner of the corrals.

An entertaining bronc ride was going on, and they watched in quiet admiration. Some of the ranch hands nodded at them, and they returned the nods.

Butch noticed that the ranch hands were unarmed. He looked around and spotted their gun belts hanging on the pole corrals.

A tall man was standing on the porch, smoking a cigar while he waited for them.

Butch glanced once more at his men, and they walked their horses past the corrals and towards the house.

Butch pulled up in front of the porch steps. His men came up beside him, and they formed a semi-circle around the porch.

It was silent for several seconds.

The tall man took a puff on his cigar as he looked them over, and their faces were emotionless as they looked back.

"You Tussle?" Butch broke the silence.

"No. I'm James Watt, the ranch foreman."

"Where's Tussle?"

"Busy," James replied, and asked, "Is there something I can do for you boys?"

Butch ignored him as he peered through the window behind James.

"Is Tussle in there?"

"He is. But, like I said; he's busy."

Butch smiled at that.

"Too busy to see the likes of us, eh?"

"I wouldn't say that," James said in a definite tone.

Butch grunted. He took a long, slow look around before returning to the ranch foreman.

"We heard you was hiring," he said in an almost mocking tone.

It was obvious that James didn't like the look of these men, and he had already dismissed the idea of hiring them.

"Was, but not now."

"You have enough hands for the drive?" Butch asked, and he tried to look hurt.

"Close enough."

"Where are they? Place looks almost deserted."

"They're around," James said patently, and added, "Is there anything else I can do for you?"

"There is," Butch smiled wolfishly at him. "We rode a long way to get here. Seems to me we could at least have a word with Mr. Tussle."

"I do the hiring and firing," James said firmly. "Now, if you'll excuse me-."

"You want us to leave?"

"Yes. We have nothing more to discuss."

"I think you're right," Butch agreed.

Soon as he said that, Butch palmed his Colt in one, quick, easy motion.

James didn't have any time to react. Butch's six-shooter roared, and the bullet hit James in the chest. The impact threw his body backwards, and he went through the open doorway and hit the floor on his back.

77

"Half of you take care of them!" Butch gestured at the corrals.

Some of the men wheeled their horses around and charged the corrals. Meanwhile, Butch dove off his horse and fired through the window at a running form.

Chapter twenty-three

Rondo, Lee, and Brian had been on Tussle's range for two days now, riding in from the south.

The country was mainly open with small, rolling hills and some mesquite bushes spread about. It had rained more than usual during spring, and the native grass was tall and green.

The sun was just beginning to go down when they spotted Tussle's ranch headquarters. It was in the far distance, and the corrals and houses merged together into one form.

"There it is," Rondo pointed.

"Hope we didn't miss supper," Lee added wistfully.

"We'll know soon enough."

"Look," Brian pointed.

Way to the west, they could see a huge herd of cattle.

"Good. They haven't left yet," Rondo looked pleased. "Now I can talk to Tussle about that job."

Lee nodded as they trotted on.

To their surprise, the past few weeks had been peaceful.

Several times they had stopped on higher ground and watched behind them. Once Rondo even slipped out and rode in a big circle, looking for tracks, but there were none to be found.

They were still wary. Rock had a reputation to live up to, and they knew they hadn't seen the last of him.

"Looks like Tussle has a big herd this year," Brian commented.

"Sure does," Rondo agreed, and he turned his horse towards the west. "Let's have a look."

"What about supper?" Lee objected.

"It can wait."

Lee mumbled his displeasure as he followed after Rondo. Brian was leading No-see-ums, and he brought up the rear.

They rode in silence as they climbed a gentle slope. When they reached the top, Lee narrowed his eyes and gestured to the south.

"Tussle has company," he announced.

A group of riders were huddled together underneath some tall cottonwoods. It was obvious that they didn't want to be seen.

They pulled up.

Lee turned in his saddle, rummaged through his saddlebags, and pulled out his eyeglass. He turned back around and looked through it.

"I count nineteen," he finally said, and he jumped in the saddle. "Rock is down there! Looks like he's leading them."

"You're sure?" Rondo asked, startled.

"It's him."

"What is he doing here?" Rondo wondered.

"Probably looking for us."

Before Rondo could reply, six of the riders left out in a trot, going towards the herd. The others stayed put underneath the trees.

Lee looked through the eyeglass again, and when he spoke his voice was grim.

"They just pulled their rifles out," he said. "Looks like they're expecting trouble."

"Or about to make some," Rondo added.

"Think they're going to hit the herd?" Brian asked.

"I'd say so," Rondo said.

"But why would Rock do that? I thought he was after us."

"Looks like he's moved on to bigger things," Rondo mused.

"What are we gonna do?" Lee asked as he returned his eyeglass to his saddlebags.

"Stop it, if we can," Rondo replied.

Lee looked at Rondo as if he'd gone crazy.

"There's nineteen of them," he objected.

"I heard you."

"Nineteen against three ain't exactly in our favor."

"Better than twenty."

Lee snorted, but didn't reply.

"You can stay here, if'n you want," Rondo offered.

"You're going, no matter what?" Lee looked at him.

"I reckon I am."

"And you?" Lee looked at Brian.

Brian nodded, and Lee sighed.

"All right then," he grumbled, and added, "We all gotta be crazy to attempt this."

"Don't have to be, but it would certainly help," Rondo agreed.

It was silent as they pulled out their weapons and checked them.

Lee and Rondo returned their rifles to their scabbards, but Brian kept ahold of his.

"We'll have to leave him," Rondo nodded at No-see-ums.

Brian dismounted and hobbled No-see-ums so that he wouldn't drift too far, and he climbed back into the saddle and nodded at Rondo.

Rondo nodded back and looked at Lee.

"You ready?"

"Not really."

"Let's go then."

They kicked up their horses to a slow trot and rode down the slope.

"This is going to end in a nasty gunfight," Lee figured.

"Looking that way in a hurry," Rondo agreed.

81

"As usual, you're dragging me and Brian right into the middle of it."

"You got a problem with that?" Rondo looked sideways at him.

"If I get a problem, you'll be the first to know."

"I usually am."

"Am what?" Lee frowned.

"The first to know."

Lee grunted, and they didn't say anything else as they trotted on.

Chapter twenty-four

There were nine ranch hands with the herd, plus the cook. They had the herd bedded down, their camp made, and a poker game just getting started.

They had drawn straws earlier, and the two losers were with the herd. They would switch with two more losers at midnight.

The cook had just finished cleaning up after supper, and he was now stirring the coals. There was a pot of coffee off to the side, just close enough to keep the brew warm.

From the poker game, a cow-puncher asked, "Pour me a cup of that, will you?"

The cook grunted his displeasure.

Before he could reply, they heard the sound of several horses approaching.

"Hello the camp!"

The poker game came to an abrupt halt.

Everybody was on their feet, reaching for their Colts and rifles when six riders rode up to camp. They were hard looking men, especially the leader.

They didn't wait for an invitation. They rode in close, dismounted, and formed a line in front of them.

The cow-punchers glanced uncertainly at each other. It was silent for only a few seconds, but it felt longer.

"Haven't seen you boys around these parts," one of the cow-punchers finally said. "Strangers, just passing through?"

The meanest looking one of the bunch smiled wolfishly.

"No. We're hunting some cows."

"Oh?"

He walked forward a little, spread his hands over the warmth of the coals, and grinned at the cook.

"Coffee smells good."

"Help yourself," the cook offered.

"Later," he said as he glanced over at the cow-punchers. "That's a big gathering of beef out there."

"Sure is," one of the cow-punchers agreed.

"Whose brand is on them?"

"J.T. Tussle's."

He smiled, looked back at his companions, and nodded.

"Who are you?" The cow-puncher asked suspiciously.

"That's not important."

"Perhaps you fellas should ride on," the cow-puncher suggested.

"Naw. Don't think so."

"You won't leave?"

He didn't reply, and a few tense seconds passed.

He straightened back up slowly. His eyes were dark as he stared at the cow-puncher.

The cow-puncher was about to speak when suddenly, in the far distance, a shot sounded out. It came from the direction of headquarters.

"What was that?" The cow-puncher asked.

With an easy movement, Rock Bullen palmed his Colt, jumped forward, and fired.

The cow-puncher was taken by surprise, and the slug slammed into his chest and propelled him backwards.

Rock kept walking forward.

The cook stumbled backwards, but he recovered and made a grab for his rifle. However, Rock put two slugs into him before he could bring the rifle up. The cook slammed into the chuck wagon and slid to the ground.

Gunshots exploded all around as Rock's men blasted away, and most of the cow-punchers managed to fire back.

The cow-punchers were decent shots, but they weren't professional gunmen. Two of the outlaws went down, but all but one of the cow-punchers fell.

The last cow-puncher stumbled backwards in panic. He started to turn and run, but Rock and the men filled him

84

with lead before he could. He jerked under the impact and fell over.

There was a momentarily lull, and then they heard the sound of a running horse. It was one of the night-riders, and he was charging the camp with his Colt in hand.

Rock was unmoved. He raised his Colt, took in a deep breath, aimed, and fired.

The slug hit the charging cow-puncher in the chest. He flipped backwards over his horse and hit the ground hard.

Meanwhile, on the other side of the herd, the second night-rider was concerned and anxious.

The sleepy herd was stirring, and several steers were struggling to their feet and bawling at the disturbance.

The confused night-rider didn't know whether to stay or run. He spoke softly to the cattle, trying to calm them.

Suddenly, he became aware of several riders coming up behind him. The brush was thick, and he couldn't see much.

"Who's out there?" He raised his voice.

Nobody answered.

"Speak up!"

Still no answer.

Too late, he finally spotted them. They all held rifles, and one was taking careful aim.

The man fired before he could react, and the slug hit him in the torso. He uttered a small cry as he fell from his saddle, and his horse jumped sideways as he hit the ground.

The closest yearlings were spooked, and they started to trot off. However, the riders spread out quickly and calmed the herd.

Back at camp, the men were checking on the downed cow-punchers. They were all dead, and Rock's eyes were cold and unmoving as he stared at them.

He knelt by the fire, grabbed a burning branch, and tossed it into the back of the chuck wagon. Seconds later, smoke started to appear.

"All right," he said. "Let's get out to the herd."

"What about these two?" One of the outlaws gestured at their two downed companions.

"They're dead, ain't they?"

"Yes."

"Then we can't do anything for them," Rock replied. "Let's go."

He moved to his horse.

The outlaws glanced at each other, shrugged, and followed after him.

Chapter twenty-five

Cooper stood in the corner by the window, smiling as he watched the excitement in Wyatt's face. Tussle was discussing the upcoming cattle drive, and Wyatt was listening intently to every word.

The rifle shot was loud, unexpected, and deafening. Everyone in the room jumped in surprise.

Cooper sprang from the corner and ran towards Josie and Wyatt. The glass behind him exploded as bullets came flying through the window.

"Get down!" Cooper shouted.

Wyatt, Josie, and Tussle fell from their chairs as broken glass sprinkled them. Meanwhile, Yancy and Jessica ran in from the kitchen, bent down low.

Yancy and Cooper held their Colts, and Tussle grabbed his new Winchester.

"Where's James?" Tussle gasped.

"Dead," Yancy said as he squatted next to the window beside Cooper.

More bullets came through the windows as Wyatt crawled over to Josie, and together they crawled to the farthest corner.

Jessica grabbed two rifles from the rifle cabinet and joined them. She offered one to Josie, and she grabbed it and worked the lever.

There was gunfire and screams coming from the corrals. Cooper took a peak out the window, but he ducked down as a volley of bullets splintered the window trim all around him.

"Keep down," Yancy growled.

"We've got to help the fellers at the corrals," Tussle said.

"Too late for that," Cooper said, his voice grave.

87

The shooting outside stopped. They heard some movement, and a voice called out.

"You inside! We want Tussle. Send him out and nobody else will get hurt."

Yancy glanced at Tussle, but nobody said anything.

"This is what you'll get if you stay in there!" The same voice said.

A sudden burst of shooting sent bullets thudding into the outside wall. Some of the bullets went through the windows and ricocheted dangerously.

The shooting eased up, and same voice said, "What's it going to be?"

"Seems serious, don't he," Cooper said softly.

"Does," Yancy agreed.

"I think he wants an answer."

"Let's give him one," Yancy said. He looked at Cooper and Tussle and asked, "Ready?"

They nodded. Then, together they rose up and fired a furious volley of shots out the window.

Chapter twenty-six

It was getting dark as Rock and his men rode to the herd.

There was still gunfire coming from headquarters, but that wasn't their concern. They had done their job; now they needed to move the herd.

It took some persuasion, but they finally managed to get the yearlings on their feet and moving. Even then they had to push them along, and the herd began to spread out.

Suddenly, they heard running horses coming from behind. Rock shouted a warning, and he turned in the saddle with his Colt in hand.

He spotted three men a-horseback. They were running hard, and were bent over their saddles.

Flashes of flame came from their Colts, and Rock heard solid thuds as the bullets hit flesh. From the corner of his eye, Rock saw three men fall.

Rock returned the gunfire, but they were moving too fast.

The irritated yearlings broke into a stumbling run, and in a mere matter of seconds complete confusion broke out as the herd split in several directions.

Bawling yearlings ran all around Rock's horse as he tried to find a target. But his nervous horse wouldn't stand still, and he had to fight to keep him under control.

Bullets were still whining all around him.

Rock saw another man fall, and then the man beside him screamed, threw his hands up, and disappeared underneath his horse.

Rock cursed as his horse stumbled.

He was thrown forward as his horse fought for footing. He thought he was going down, but the terrified animal somehow managed to regain his footing.

Rock pulled himself back into the saddle and looked around. Two more men had gone down, and Rock decided he'd had enough.

"Let's clear out!" He yelled.

His men needed no further encouragement.

Raking their horses with their spurs, they headed north. Spooked yearlings were still running all around, and they had to maneuver through the herd. But they finally got clear of the yearlings, and they ran their horses wide open.

Rondo, Lee, and Brian did not pursue them. Instead, they pulled up and reloaded.

"Everybody all right?" Rondo asked.

Lee and Brian nodded.

Gunfire was still coming from headquarters, and Rondo looked concerned.

"Sounds like more trouble," he said.

"Let's go have a look," Lee suggested.

Rondo took off in a lope, and Lee and Brian followed.

Chapter twenty-seven

They rode in unseen from behind the corrals.

There were lifeless bodies scattered around the corrals; all shot down unarmed. It was a sobering sight, and Rondo felt a rage building in him.

All of the gunfire was coming from the main house.

They could see several outlaws, hunkered down, firing furiously at the windows and doors. There was also steady gunfire being returned from the house.

"Tussle's putting up a fight," Lee said softly.

"Sounds like he has help," Rondo added.

"What are we gonna do?" Brian spoke up.

Rondo looked around and gestured at the herd of horses that were milling in the dry lot.

Lee and Brian understood, and they nodded curtly.

The outlaws were so intent on the house, they failed to notice as Rondo rode over to the gate and swung it open.

The terrified horses needed no encouragement. As soon as they saw the opening, they ran wildly out the gate.

With their Colts drawn, Rondo, Lee, and Brian flanked them and turned them towards the main house.

The outlaws heard the pounding of hooves. They stopped shooting, and most of them stood and spun around.

But the shooting from the house never stopped, and most of outlaws that stood were riddled with lead and flung violently to the ground.

Those that were left panicked as their horses broke free and joined in with the running horses.

They ran after their mounts, and everybody from the house fired steadily at them, as did Rondo, Lee, and Brian.

One outlaw after another went down, and the horses trampled another one.

Butch was the only one who reached his horse. The animal was terrified, but he managed to swing on.

91

Soon as he hit the saddle, the horse broke into a dead run. Bullets flew by his head, and this made the horse run even faster. Butch ducked and hung on as they made their escape.

By now the rest of the horses had cleared out, and all shooting stopped.

It was over.

Lee, Rondo, and Brian trotted their horses back to the main house, and they were surprised when Yancy and Cooper walked out, followed by Tussle, Josie, Jessica, and Wyatt.

Yancy narrowed his eyes at Lee, but nobody said anything. Instead, it was silent as everybody looked around.

It was a sobering scene. There were dead bodies scattered everywhere, both good and bad.

"Where'd you fellows come from?" Tussle finally broke the silence.

"We were trying to save your herd," Rondo explained. "We came soon as we could."

"They hit the herd too?" Tussle asked.

Rondo nodded somberly.

"How bad?"

"Bad," Rondo's voice was subdued. "We couldn't get there in time. They killed them all."

Tussle was obviously shaken, and he shook his head in disbelief as he tried to grasp the situation.

"The herd?" He asked, his voice hoarse.

"Scattered all over."

Tussle turned and walked over to the porch railing.

There was no reason to say anything; the look on Tussle's face said it all.

Chapter twenty-eight

Butch was furious.

He rode to their camp, and he was surprised to find Rock and some of the men there.

They were gathered around the campfire, drinking coffee. They looked irritated and annoyed.

"What happened?" Butch asked as he dismounted.

"We ran into a little problem," Rock said, and then he explained. "What happened at headquarters?" He asked afterwards.

Butch explained, and afterwards it was silent as everybody thought on that.

"How many men did you lose?" Butch asked after a while.

It was silent as Rock counted in his head.

"Nine."

Butch grunted his displeasure and shook his head.

"We lost nine at headquarters too," he muttered. "Eighteen men, all dead. That only leaves eleven of us."

"Tussle lost some men too," Rock added.

"Not enough," Butch grumbled. "Those fellers that were shooting at us from the main house were good. Real good."

"So, are we gonna give up?" Rock asked, and there was a mocking tone in his voice.

Butch snorted.

"You think we should?"

"I ain't the boss," Rock shrugged.

"That's right, and we ain't leaving until the job's done," Butch growled. "I want Tussle dead."

Rock smiled wryly and nodded.

"I do have a thought," he suggested.

"Your last thought didn't work out so well."

Rock ignored the sarcasm as he nodded at Sim.

"Sim here just told me that he's punched cows before."

"So?"

"Tussle's going to be mighty short handed now," Rock explained. "He'll probably hire just about anybody, even ol' Sim."

Butch pinched his face in thought but didn't say anything.

"Sim could make a hand for a few days, bide his time, and kill Tussle when nobody's looking," Rock suggested. "With Tussle out of the way, the outfit will probably fold and we can swoop in and get the herd."

"That could work," Butch said.

"Sure it will."

Butch glanced at Sim.

"You'd be willing?"

"Sure, long as the price is right," Sim said.

"You too?" Butch scowled at him.

"Feller has to look out for himself," Sim replied defensively.

Butch sighed and nodded.

"Name your price," he muttered.

Chapter twenty-nine

It was a somber night.

Everybody stayed at the main house, and nobody was in the mood to talk much.

Lee thought about approaching Jessica, but decided that now was not the time.

There was much work to do the next day.

Rondo saddled up and rode out at first light to scout for tracks. As for everybody else, they hitched up the buckboard, gathered all the bodies, and dug graves at the top of the hill in the graveyard. This took half the day, and by the time they got everybody buried it was late afternoon.

They all stood solemnly around the graves. Cooper read from his Bible, and Tussle said a prayer. His voice broke several times, and when he finished he turned towards the house. He looked defeated and lost.

Rondo rode back in at suppertime. He unsaddled, fed his horse, and joined everyone at the main house.

"Find anything?" Tussle asked as they all sat around the dinner table to eat the meal that Jessica and Josie had prepared.

Rondo shook his head.

"Too many tracks scattered out there."

"But they're gone?"

"For now," Rondo replied, and added, "That doesn't mean they won't come back."

"I hope they do," Tussle grunted.

"I did see several big bunches of yearlings," Rondo continued. "It shouldn't take much to get most of them gathered back up."

"How am I supposed to do that?" Tussle asked sourly.

"You can't hire another crew?"

"Not this late in the year," Tussle muttered. "Anybody worth having has already hired on with some other outfit."

"That's actually why I'm here, was to see about a job," Rondo said.

"You're hired," Tussle declared, and added, "But the two of us can't take a herd of yearlings to Kansas."

"Three," Wyatt spoke up.

Cooper and Josie were startled, and they stared wide-eyed at Wyatt.

Tussle looked at Wyatt and smiled faintly.

"Brian and I could help," Lee spoke up, and Brian nodded.

"I appreciate that, but five ain't enough either."

Lee started to reply, but Jessica spoke before he could.

"No," she said, her voice cold.

"What?" Tussle scowled at his niece.

"I don't want him working for us."

"Why not?" Tussle demanded to know.

"I have my reasons."

"Jessica," Lee spoke back up, and his voice was gentle. "I don't blame you for hating me, but Brian and I rode all this way just to see you. If we could talk in private, you'll feel different."

"No," Yancy entered the conversation, and his voice was firm. "Anything you got to say, you say it here."

"This is between me, Brian, and Jessica," Lee shot Yancy a dark look. "Stay out of it."

"Whatever you have to say, I don't want to hear it," Jessica declared.

"You'll want to hear this," Lee objected.

"All I want is for you to leave."

Tussle suddenly slammed the palm of his hand down on the table, and all the glassware and dishes rattled. Everyone was startled, and they looked at Tussle.

"Now is not the time to work out everybody's relationship problems," he growled, and added, "I rode with Lee during the war, and you won't find anybody more loyal. He saved my life more than once. If he wants a job, then he has it, and that's final."

Yancy frowned while Jessica crossed her arms.

"Fine," she said stiffly, and she glared at Lee. "You might work here, but stay away from me."

"I'm sorry, but we have to talk," Lee replied. "It's important."

Yancy leaned forward in his chair and looked Lee in the eyes.

"You heard her," he said in a low, somber voice. "Stay away from her, or you'll have me to answer to."

Lee was unmoved by Yancy's warning, and he narrowed his eyes as they looked at each other.

"Next time we face each other," Lee said softly. "I'll make sure your brother isn't backing you up from behind a window."

The muscles in Yancy's jaw rippled. He didn't say anything, and the silence was tense.

Several seconds passed before Cooper cleared his throat and changed the subject.

"What are you going to do, Tussle? About the cattle drive, I mean."

"What can I do? I reckon I'll borrow more money and wait until next year."

"There's a man named John Lytle in town," Cooper commented. "He's a trail driver."

"I've heard of him," Tussle scowled. "You give him half the herd, and he'll make the drive to Kansas for you."

"Not quite half," Cooper corrected. "I could talk to him, if you wanted."

It fell silent as Tussle thought on it, and he finally sighed and nodded.

"It wouldn't hurt to see what he has to say," he said.

"All right," Cooper said. "We'll ride back to town in the morning."

Tussle nodded and turned to Brian.

97

"You might as well go with them. Ask around, and see if you can find anybody who's a decent hand that wants a job."

"Sure thing," Brian said.

"Now, if we could," Tussle said. "Let's eat supper without anymore bickering, and then we'd best get to bed. We've a lot of work to do tomorrow."

Lee looked at Jessica, but she ignored him. Next, he looked at Yancy, and several seconds passed as they stared at each other.

"I can do that," Lee said softly.

Yancy took in a deep breath, exhaled, and nodded.

"Me too," he said.

Chapter thirty

Yancy, Cooper, and Brian rode out at daybreak. As for everybody else, they rode out and gathered the remuda back up.

This took most of the morning, and they spent the rest of the day picking out their string of horses. A few of the horses needed shoeing, and there were still a few that needed topping off.

Yancy, Cooper, and Brian rode back in late afternoon, and another man trailed along behind them.

He looked to be in his mid-thirties. He seemed very comfortable in a saddle, and he had stooped shoulders and long legs. He was thin, and his eyes were watchful and sharp.

They pulled up at the corrals, and Cooper introduced him.

"Tussle, this is John T. Lytle."

Tussle nodded slowly as he looked him over.

"Trail driver, eh?"

John used a thumb to shove his hat brim up, and then he smiled. His face was warm and friendly.

"Yes, sir. That's what I do."

"You hoping to cash in on our misfortunes?" Tussle spoke bluntly.

"Not at all. Coop told me what happened, and I thought I could help."

"How?"

"We're heading to Kansas in a few weeks," John explained. "Right now, we're in the process of pooling several small herds together at Fort Worth. All you'd have to do is get your herd there."

Tussle looked thoughtful.

"It's a two week drive to Fort Worth," he figured.

"Sounds about right," John agreed.

99

"If we could leave in the next day or two, we'd make it," Tussle said, and added, "Course, I'd have to find some help."

Cooper glanced at Yancy. He nodded, so Cooper cleared his throat.

"We talked it over, Tussle, and you can count us in."

Tussle was surprised.

"But you're both Texas Rangers," he pointed out.

"I never did get to take that furlough a while back," Cooper replied. "'Bout time I did."

"I appreciate that," Tussle said earnestly.

Yancy and Cooper nodded, and it was silent as Tussle counted to himself.

"Including Wyatt, that makes seven," he said. "We'd be spread thin, but it's doable."

"Don't forget about Josie," Cooper said. "She can ride good as any man."

"I'm going too," Jessica spoke up.

"Absolutely not!" Tussle bellowed, and everyone was startled by his outburst.

"Why not?" Cooper asked.

"I will not have women on my drive," Tussle declared. "It's not proper."

"I understand your concerns, but Josie grew up with the Apaches," Cooper reminded. "She's not like most women."

"Neither am I!" Jessica glared at her Uncle.

Tussle didn't reply. Instead, he turned back to John.

"How long will this drive of yours to Kansas take?"

"'Bout three months," John replied. "Long as the grass is good, we don't get in any hurry. We let 'em graze as they walk."

His comments pleased Tussle, and he suddenly looked hopeful.

"What'll it cost me?" He asked.

John named a price. It was more than fair, and Tussle agreed.

100

"All right. We'll be there soon as we can."

"Send word if you run into trouble," John said. "We'll wait long as we can."

"We'll be along," Tussle nodded.

"I'd stay and help," John added, "but I've got to get back to Forth Worth."

"Don't worry about us," Tussle replied. "We'll be fine."

"Well, good luck," John said. He said goodbye and kicked up his horse.

They stood there and watched him leave, and Tussle looked thoughtful.

"I don't even have a cook," he commented.

"I can cook," Josie offered.

"No!" Yancy and Cooper exclaimed.

Josie shot them a dark look, but Tussle spoke again before she could reply.

"I'll do the cooking," he decided. "There's an old chuck wagon in the barn we can take."

Everybody looked concerned, and Cooper asked, "Can you cook?"

"We'll find out," Tussle replied, and he looked at Brian. "Find anybody in town?"

Brian shook his head.

"There was only one fellow wanting a job, but he was green."

"How green?"

"He thought a saddle horn was a musical instrument."

Tussle groaned. He glanced at Jessica, and she was still glaring at him, as was Josie.

"Are you two determined to come along?" He asked.

They nodded.

"This ain't going to be a Sunday picnic," he warned. "There'll be no baths or outhouses on this trip."

Neither one replied, and Tussle sighed.

"Fine," he murmured. "You can come along."

Jessica and Josie were pleased, and they smiled.

Tussle muttered as he headed towards the main house. "Lord, have mercy," everyone heard him say.

Chapter thirty-one

Everybody sat out on the front porch that evening after supper. Jessica sat as far away from Lee as possible, and the talk was mostly pleasant.

The sun was going down when they spotted a rider trotting towards headquarters.

Nobody said anything. However, everyone shifted in their chairs so that their six-shooters were more accessible if need be.

He came up by the corrals, passed the bunkhouse, and pulled up in front of the main house.

It was silent as everybody studied him. He was an older man, probably close to Brian Clark's age.

"Howdy," he finally said.

"Looking for something?" Tussle spoke frankly.

The older man smiled and nodded.

"Was hoping for a job."

Tussle looked intrigued.

"Ever punch cows before?"

"Sure."

"Been on any cattle drives?"

"Some."

"We're leaving on a cattle drive in a few days," Tussle said. "Going to Fort Worth."

"Sounds fine."

Tussle had a few more questions.

"Where you from?"

"East."

"What'd you do back east?" Tussle prompted.

The man shrugged.

"A little bit of everything."

"Ever been in these parts before?"

"Nope."

"What are you doing here now?"

"Riding the grub line, looking for work," he said. He smiled and asked, "Anymore questions?"

"Sure. What's your name?"

"Sim. Sim Haine."

Tussle nodded and introduced everyone, and Sim's eyes grew wider with each name.

"I've heard of all you fellas," he said. He looked at Tussle and asked, "You expecting trouble?"

"Mebbe."

"Well, I'd say you're prepared for it."

Tussle grunted in response and gestured at the bunkhouse.

"You can sleep in there," he said. "Put your horse up in the barn, and you can pick out a string in the morning. You had supper?"

"Yes, sir."

"Good. We'll be leaving out at first light."

"I'll be ready," Sim said, and he nodded at everyone and turned his horse toward the barn.

Soon as he was out of earshot, Cooper turned to Yancy and murmured, "He doesn't talk much."

Yancy nodded.

"That's what I like about him," he replied.

Chapter thirty-two

They rode out the next morning.

Rondo led the drive. He spread everybody out, and they gathered the country to the north.

Tussle and Wyatt stayed at headquarters. They pulled the old chuck wagon out of the barn and gave it a good going over.

First, they cleared out all the cobwebs in the cupboard drawers. They greased the wheels, mended the tarp, replaced split boards, and tar-caulked the bottom.

Tussle took his time. This was an important job, because the chuck wagon was going be their home until the cattle drive was over.

Once the supplies were loaded, they hitched up the team and left headquarters. They could see a herd coming together in the distance, and they went to a lakebed that was close by and made camp.

Tussle sent Wyatt after some firewood, and he gathered a big pile of mesquite wood. Tussle built a fire, and soon he had coals ready to cook with.

They drifted in that evening, except for Sim and Rondo. They were with the herd, and they wouldn't come in until they were relieved.

"Get it while it's hot," Tussle called out.

Everybody looked somber as they formed a line.

Tussle stood beside the chuck wagon, and his face was harsh as he waited for somebody to say something.

"What's for supper?" Cooper asked.

"Eat it and find out," Tussle replied gruffly. "And you can pour your own coffee."

Everybody filed past Tussle, and they filled their tin plates with a ladle full of beans.

"No meat?" Cooper scowled.

"No, and you boys can wash your own plates too."

Cooper looked around, but spotted no washtub.

"With what?"

"Just rub your plates out with sand. That's what I do."

Cooper didn't reply. He walked over and sat beside Yancy and murmured, "Some furlough we've decided to take."

"You can sure pick 'em," Yancy replied. "Going to the mountains, and now this."

Cooper grunted his response.

Night settled over the camp as they ate their beans. Afterwards, Lee and Brian rode out to relieve Rondo and Sim.

"How many head you figure we gathered today?" Tussle asked as he served Rondo a plate full of beans.

Rondo studied his plate with a thoughtful frown.

"I'd say a little over a thousand. We got lucky and found some big bunches today."

"Good," Tussle nodded. "If we can gather that many tomorrow, then we can head out."

Rondo nodded. He walked over and sat beside Cooper, and then somberly started in on his beans.

Jessica and Josie sat together, away from the men.

They had worked hard and were exhausted. However, neither one would admit it.

"Long day," Jessica started a conversation.

"Yes," Josie replied, and added, "But, there will be longer."

"I'd better get accustomed to it then," Jessica said, and her eyes twinkled.

Josie nodded and smiled politely.

"We've never had the opportunity to talk much," Jessica said, and added, "You sure have been through a lot this past year."

"So have you."

106

"I guess I have," Jessica agreed. It was silent, and then she asked, "So, how do you like being married to a Landon?"

Josie thought for a moment.

"Better than being married to an Indian."

"Yes, I imagine so," Jessica smiled.

"Cooper is a good man," Josie declared, and added, "So is Yancy."

"Yes, they are," Jessica agreed, and then she asked nonchalantly, "Do you know Yancy very well?"

"He doesn't talk much. Neither do I or Wyatt."

"But Cooper likes to talk."

"He does."

"So Cooper does the talking for everybody?"

"Pretty much."

Jessica frowned as she thought on that.

"I guess I like to talk," she admitted, and added, "That is, except for whenever I'm around Yancy. I can't seem to think straight, and he never says anything either."

"Silence is Yancy's friend."

Jessica grunted and looked across the camp at him.

"Well, I hope they're happy together," she pouted.

Chapter thirty-three

Wyatt rode out with the men the next morning. Tussle stayed in camp, and Jessica and Josie stayed with the herd.

Rondo led the drive again. They went west several miles, and they scattered out and rode back towards the herd.

By noon they had gathered another big bunch of yearlings. They drove them back to the herd, and then everybody but Yancy and Cooper rode to camp.

Tussle had more beans prepared, and this time nobody said anything as they filled their plates.

"Roughly speaking, I'd say we have close to two thousand head," Rondo told Tussle.

Tussle nodded, pleased.

"That's good enough," he declared. He paused and added, "I sure hate to leave headquarters deserted."

"What other choices are there?" Rondo replied.

"I reckon there aren't any," Tussle said, and then he changed the subject. "Do you know the country between here and Fort Worth?"

"Some."

"You'll be our scout then," Tussle decided. "You've done it before, and you know what to do."

Rondo nodded, and his face looked thoughtful.

"We'll pass by Big Spring, Sweetwater, and Abilene. We can get supplies at any of those towns."

"It depends on how many beans you boys eat," Tussle grunted.

"Much rain as we've had this spring, the grass should be good all the way," Rondo continued. "As for water, there should be plenty of full lakebeds and a few streams."

"What about Indians?" Jessica spoke up. "Do you think we'll run into any?"

Rondo looked at her, and she seemed more curious than frightened.

"It's possible," he said.

"There's also the bunch that attacked us," Tussle reminded. "They could show back up."

Sim glanced up from across the camp, and there was a hint of a smile on his face. But it disappeared when he noticed Rondo watching him.

"It's possible," Rondo said again.

Chapter thirty-four

Yancy liked to practice with his six-shooter every few weeks. It kept him sharp and prepared.

Rondo and Brian were with the herd that afternoon, and everybody else was lounging around camp, mending any gear that needed it.

"I'll be back in a while," Yancy told Tussle, and he climbed on his horse.

Lee watched him ride out and glanced at Cooper. "Where's he going?"

Cooper explained, and Lee nodded and stood.

"Think I'll go have a talk with him."

"He likes to practice alone," Cooper warned.

"He'll get over it," Lee smiled.

He walked over to his horse, mounted up, and trotted out.

Lee could see Yancy in the distance. He wasn't in any hurry, and Lee trotted slowly as he followed.

Yancy rode a few miles and pulled up at a cluster of trees. Lee trotted up as he was hobbling his horse.

Yancy straightened back up, and it was silent as they looked at each other.

Lee didn't say anything. He just waited.

Finally, Yancy said, "I came out here to shoot."

"I know."

"You followed me," Yancy said, and it sounded more like a statement than a question.

"I did, yes."

"Weren't being very sneaky about it," Yancy frowned. "I spotted you right off."

"I wasn't trying to be sneaky. I came out here to talk."

"You're always wanting to talk."

Lee chuckled softly at that.

"I always irritate you, don't I."

"Mostly."

"Good," Lee grinned.

Yancy grunted. A few seconds passed, and then he sighed.

"Care to join me?"

"What are we going to use as targets?" Lee asked wryly.

"What do you want to use?" Yancy played along.

"We already tried each other," Lee reminded.

"I was thinking we could shoot at them," Yancy nodded at the cluster of trees.

"I'll agree to that," Lee said.

He dismounted, hobbled his horse, and walked up beside Yancy.

"You go first," Lee offered.

Yancy shook his head.

"You don't trust me?" Lee tried to look insulted.

"You really want me to answer that?"

Lee smiled, and said, "Let's shoot together then."

"All right."

They stood side by side, facing the trees, and several seconds passed.

Suddenly, in the blink of an eye, they palmed their Colts, and their shots blended together as they fired in rapid fashion.

Afterwards, they were silent. They reloaded their Colts, holstered them, and walked over to the trees.

Both spreads were as small as a clenched fist.

"We're good," Lee observed.

"We are," Yancy agreed.

"Nice, how you held your Colt sideways."

"I've been working on that."

"You only fired five shots," Lee said wryly.

"So did you."

"Never hurts to be careful."

"It doesn't," Yancy agreed.

111

Lee smiled at that and walked forward. He rested his hand on a tree as he looked at the far horizon.

"I need to talk to Jessica," he said plainly.

Yancy frowned and studied Lee for several moments.

"We already discussed this."

"We have," Lee nodded.

Yancy took in a deep breath and let it out slowly.

"What's it all about?"

"That's between me and her. And Brian."

"I know you lost her money."

Lee was surprised. He turned from the tree and looked at Yancy.

"She didn't want anybody to know about that."

"Well, she told me."

"I didn't lose it on purpose," Lee said. "It just happened, and it's been eating at me ever since."

"Well, that's all in the past. There's no use talking about it anymore."

"But I got the hotel back," Lee explained. "Or, at least Jessica's part of it."

"Hotel? What hotel?"

Lee narrowed his eyes.

"I thought you said you knew."

"I knew about the money."

Lee sighed, and Yancy waited.

"We invested her money into a hotel," Lee explained. "A very fancy hotel. You've heard of The Palace Hotel in Empty-lake?"

Yancy nodded.

"Me, Brian, and Jessica were the owners until I lost it in a poker game. But then, I got Jessica's half back. Jeremiah Wisdom owns the other half."

"Jeremiah?" Yancy's eyes grew wide. "What's he got to do with this?"

"Plenty," Lee grumbled. "Anyhow, that's why we're here, is to tell Jessica."

112

"What's in it for you and Brian?"

"Nothing. Soon as Jessica knows, we're out of it."

Yancy looked displeased as he thought on it.

"I'll tell her," he said.

"I was hoping you would."

"Well, we'd best be getting back," Yancy said abruptly.

Lee nodded. They walked over to their horses, untied them, climbed on, and took out in a trot.

It was obvious that Yancy was irritated, but Lee still had one more matter to discuss.

"I almost forgot," Lee said.

Yancy glanced sideways at him.

"Yes?"

"My pardon."

"What about it?"

"Me and Brian held up our end of the agreement," Lee reminded.

"I know that."

"Well then?"

"You'll get your pardons soon enough."

"How soon?"

"Soon as I see Judge Parker."

"And when will that be?" Lee pressed.

"Soon as the cattle drive is over."

"I'd appreciate that."

"Don't mention it."

Lee nodded, and no more words were spoken as they rode back.

Chapter thirty-five

As soon as Yancy and Lee rode out, Sim asked to go to town.

"What for?" Tussle demanded.

"Thought I'd take a bath and get a shave," Sim said. "I could sure use one."

"No need to go to town for that," Tussle replied. "There's a stock tank you can use just to the south of here."

Sim smiled.

"I could also use a drink. Be my last one for a while."

Tussle narrowed his eyes.

"You a drinking man?"

"Some."

Tussle grunted his displeasure, and it was silent as he thought on it.

"I won't be gone long," Sim added.

"You'd better not," Tussle replied. "We leave at daybreak."

"I'll be back."

Tussle grunted again while Sim untied his horse and stepped into the saddle.

***

Sim rode north, but he didn't go to town. Instead, he rode to Butch's camp.

The camp was well hidden, and Sim had some trouble finding it again. They heard him coming, and they were waiting with their Colts in hand as he rode up. But then Butch recognized him, and everyone relaxed.

"Kill Tussle yet?" Butch looked hopeful.

"No."

"Why not?"

"Do you have any idea who he's got working for him?"

114

"Who?"

Sim told them, and everybody was startled.

"So, it was the Landons we were going up against," Butch said thoughtfully.

"It sure was. And, you are mistaken if you think I'm going to take them all on by myself."

"What are Tussle's plans?" Butch asked as he ignored his comments.

Sim explained, and Rock and Butch looked at each other.

"Can Tussle cook?" Rock spoke up.

"No, he's horrible."

Rock grinned wolfishly and asked, "You say he's short handed?"

"Sure is," Sim nodded.

"It's simple then," Butch spoke back up. "All you have to do is wait until Tussle is alone at the chuck wagon. You can take care of him and clear out."

"And then have the Landons after me?" Sim scowled. "I wouldn't stand a chance."

"You would if you led them into an ambush," Rock spoke up, and suggested, "We could ride on up ahead and be waiting for you."

"That might actually work," Butch agreed, and he looked at Sim. "What do you say?"

"I'm still the one taking all the risks," Sim objected.

It was silent for a moment, and Butch nodded.

"All right," he said. "I'll send some more men to see Tussle in a few days. Short handed as he is, he'll probably take them on. Then you won't be alone when you face Tussle."

Sim was silent as he thought it over.

"What about the herd?" He asked.

"After we ambush the Landons, you boys can ride back and pick them up."

"That might work," Sim said thoughtfully.

"Sure it will," Butch said, and added, "We'll ride on ahead past Abilene and find us a good spot. We'll be waiting for you there."

Sim nodded and turned his horse.

"I'll see you in a few days," he said.

Butch nodded, and they stood there and watched as Sim trotted out.

Chapter thirty-six

Camp was quiet that evening after supper.

It was Yancy and Cooper's turn to be with the herd, and everybody else lingered around camp. Rondo drank coffee while Lee smoked a cigar.

"Let's play poker," Lee suggested.

"I don't have any money," Rondo shrugged.

Lee frowned. He looked around camp, and his face lit up.

"We can use cow chips."

"Cow chips?"

"Sure, and the winners can burn their winnings."

Rondo chuckled.

"Let's just use matches," he suggested.

Rondo, Brian, and Lee started a game while Josie and Wyatt watched. As for Jessica, she stayed on the other side of camp and ignored Lee.

They had only played a few hands when they heard someone trotting up. It was Sim, and he tended to his horse and walked up to camp. He smiled and tried to look unconcerned.

Tussle frowned at him.

"I thought you wanted a bath and shave," he said gruffly.

Sim was startled.

"How about that!" He exclaimed. "I reckon I forgot."

"I bet you didn't forget that drink."

"No, didn't forget that," Sim grinned.

Tussle grunted, and Sim grabbed his coffee cup and moved towards the fire.

Rondo watched him thoughtfully from across camp.

"I don't trust him," he said softly.

"That's the Landon way," Lee replied as he studied his cards. "You folks don't trust anybody."

117

"I trust you," Rondo pointed out.

"Yancy doesn't," Lee said, and added, "Now, if you don't mind, can we get back to the game? I have a good hand here."

"I fold then," Rondo's eyes twinkled.

"Me too," Brian tossed his cards down.

Lee grumbled, gathered the cards, and shuffled.

They played for several hours, and then they rolled out their bedrolls and crawled in.

A few minutes later, everybody but Lee had drifted to sleep.

While Brian snored beside him, Lee lay on his back and thought about the cattle drive and the situation with Jessica and Yancy.

He finally decided to stop thinking about it, and his thoughts drifted to April and June.

He wondered if April ever thought about him, and then he speculated on how friendly she and Jeremiah Wisdom had become.

Lee sighed wistfully and decided not to think about that either.

Chapter thirty-seven

It was decided that Lee and Brian would be the horse wranglers.

It was a full time job. They had to take care of the remuda and keep them up with the herd.

On most cattle drives, cow-punchers usually changed horses twice a day. But, short handed as they were, Tussle figured they would wear out more horses than that.

Everybody took their places the next morning.

The yearlings were restless, and they didn't need much encouragement to move out. Tussle rode in the chuck wagon, and he was off to the side of the herd.

Rondo helped get the drive started, and then he trotted on ahead to scout. That left Yancy, Cooper, Wyatt, Sim, Jessica, and Josie with the main herd.

Jessica was at the back, riding drag and pushing up the slower moving yearlings.

Yancy flanked the herd to Jessica's left. He kept glancing back, and after a while he rode over to her.

"You all right back here?" He asked.

"I'm fine, thank you."

Yancy nodded and fell in beside her.

"Dusty back here," he commented.

"It is," she agreed.

Yancy nodded again, and it fell silent as he tried to think of something to say.

"Been a busy few days," he finally said.

"It sure has," Jessica replied, and added, "I can't understand how everyone is handling it so well."

"Handling what?"

"We almost died a few days ago," Jessica reminded. "Our friends were killed. Murdered. And yet everyone acts as if nothing happened."

Yancy nodded, almost apologetically.

119

"I reckon it's because we're all so accustomed to death," he said. "Coop and I have been around it since before the war."

"How can you ever get accustomed to all the killing?"

"Repetition helps," Yancy replied matter-of-factly. "First time I killed a man, it bothered me for a while. Now I don't mind so much. Especially if they need killing."

"How do you decide if they need killing?" Jessica looked at him.

A faint smile crossed his face.

"Most of the time, it's easy to tell."

"Like when they attacked the ranch," Jessica said.

"Yes, like that."

Jessica nodded as she thought on that.

"Well, you are good at it," she said. "You, and everybody else."

"We've had plenty of practice."

"Do you plan on being a lawman forever?" Jessica changed the subject.

Yancy was surprised by the question.

"Never really thought on it much," he admitted.

"It's a dangerous life."

"It is, sometimes," Yancy agreed, and added, "Punching cows can be dangerous too."

"But cows don't shoot at you."

"No, but they can sure run you over."

Jessica laughed. It was silent for a bit, and she suddenly smiled.

"This is the longest conversation we've ever had," she pointed out.

Yancy was startled.

"Yes," he said thoughtfully. "I believe it is."

"Maybe we can do it again sometime," Jessica suggested.

"I'd like that," Yancy said. A thought occurred to him, and he asked, "How 'bout tonight? There is something I'd like to discuss."

Excitement filled Jessica's face.

"After supper?"

"That'll be fine," Yancy agreed.

He tipped his hat at her and kicked up his horse.

Jessica watched him go, and she smiled to herself as she moved over and pushed up a slower moving yearling.

She glanced at the sun and frowned impatiently.

Supper couldn't get here fast enough.

Chapter thirty-eight

Rondo rode back in as it was getting dark, and he passed by the herd on his way to camp.

Sim and Josie were the night-riders, and Rondo frowned at that. He nodded at Josie as he trotted by.

After tending to his horse, he filled his plate with beans and sat down. He sipped his scalding hot coffee and looked around camp at everyone.

"We made good time today," he commented.

"I'd say so," Yancy agreed.

"I rode several miles ahead," he said. "Grass is good, and there's plenty of water."

"See any tracks?" Tussle wanted to know.

"Some."

"Injuns?"

"Looked like," Rondo nodded. "But, they were several days old and moving to the south."

Tussle grunted his approval as he put more wood on the fire.

"Sure is a pleasant night," Cooper commented from across the fire. "I hope the weather holds for the next few weeks."

"My aching joints tells me it's going to rain," Lee spoke up.

"Aching joints?" Brian looked Lee and scowled. "Live another twenty years, and then come talk to me about aching joints."

"Lee does have a point," Cooper spoke up. "I killed a rattlesnake today, and he turned belly up."

"Not that again," Yancy sighed, and he gestured at the clear, black sky. "It's not going to rain tonight, I can tell you that."

Rondo smiled at the conversation. He stood, walked over to the fire, and poured another cup of coffee.

"I noticed Josie is with Sim," Rondo commented.

"That's right," Tussle nodded.

"Wyatt's about to relieve her," Cooper spoke up. "She wanted him to eat some beans – I mean – supper first."

Tussle scowled at Cooper but didn't say anything.

"I hadn't had the chance to mention it, but I think we should keep an eye on Sim," Rondo said.

Everybody nodded in agreement, except for Lee and Tussle.

"He might pull a cork every now and then, but he seems all right to me," Tussle said. "He works hard."

"There's just something about him," Rondo replied. "I've seen it before."

Lee scowled, but Tussle shrugged.

"Fine by me," he said. "Watch him all you want."

Rondo nodded, and it fell silent. A few minutes passed, and Jessica looked anxious.

"I feel like going for a walk," she finally said. She turned to Yancy and asked, "Will you come with me?"

Yancy's face turned red, but he still nodded.

"I'd like that," he said.

Nobody dared to snicker as they stood and walked out into the darkness.

Soon as they were gone, Cooper and Rondo looked at each other.

"Interesting," Rondo said.

"Yes," Cooper agreed. "Very."

Chapter thirty-nine

The night air was cool and crisp. There was a gentle breeze, and the sounds of the night were loud.

They were silent as they strolled along side by side. They both had things to say, but neither one was in any hurry to say them.

Yancy didn't want to startle the herd, so they walked in the opposite direction. Several minutes passed, and then Jessica cleared her throat.

"Would you ever consider becoming a cowman?"

Again, Yancy was surprised by her question.

"Sure," he smiled. "All I need is a ranch and some cows."

"You could work for my Uncle," Jessica suggested. "He's very fond of you all. Especially Wyatt."

Yancy turned and studied Jessica with thoughtful eyes, and he didn't say anything for a long time.

"I like being a Ranger," he finally said in a quiet voice. "I'm good at it."

"But Tussle needs a new ranch foreman," Jessica objected.

"Rondo seems to be taking that position."

"But he's so young!"

"He can handle it."

Jessica sighed and looked frustrated.

"Don't you understand? Tussle needs somebody to come along side of him. Someone who can take over the ranch someday. Someone like you."

Yancy frowned.

"Is that what you want?" He asked.

"Yes," Jessica said. "I want that for us. I want a place to settle down and raise a family."

"Cooper and Josie don't seem to be having any trouble."

124

"Josie is different," Jessica replied. "She doesn't mind moving around all the time."

"And you would?"

It was silent as she thought on that.

"I'm not sure," she finally said.

Yancy frowned, and it fell silent again as they walked on.

"I got a message to deliver," Yancy changed the subject.

"Oh? From who?"

"Lee."

Jessica's face turned dark.

"What does he want?"

"He and Brian got your hotel back. Or, at least your part."

"What?" Jessica was startled. "How'd they do that?"

"You'd have to ask them."

Jessica uttered a short laugh and shook her head in wonder.

"How about that!" She exclaimed.

"Yes, how 'bout that," Yancy said, and his voice carried no emotion.

She glanced at him and noticed his sour look.

"You don't seem very happy about it."

"I reckon I'm not."

"Why not?"

Yancy sighed.

"It's complicated."

"How so?"

"I'm not sure I got the words to make you understand."

"You could try," Jessica prompted.

Yancy didn't reply, and Jessica was suddenly irritated.

"We'd best head back," she said, and there was anger in her voice.

"We probably should," Yancy agreed.

They turned back toward camp, and it was silent as they walked back.

Chapter forty

Everybody looked up as Yancy and Jessica came in from the darkness. Nobody said anything, and their curiosity sharpened when they noticed the sour looks on their faces.

It was time to turn in.

Yancy rolled his bedroll out next to Cooper, and his movements were abrupt and jerky.

Cooper was lying in his bedroll, his hands clasped behind his head, as he watched Yancy.

"Have a nice walk?" He asked.

Yancy grunted and crawled in his bedroll. It was silent for a bit, and Yancy rolled over.

"I'm hungry," he said. "And I'm sick of beans."

"It's just your imagination," Cooper replied. "Go to sleep, and you'll be fine."

"I don't think I *can* sleep on an empty stomach."

"Sleep on your back then."

Yancy scowled but didn't reply.

A few seconds passed, and Cooper sighed as he looked up at the clear, dark sky.

"Living in town, it's easy to forget what it's like to sleep outdoors," he said, and added, "Those stars are beautiful."

"I can walk outside and look at stars anytime," Yancy objected.

"But it's not the same as sleeping under them."

"I'll take my bed in my house. You can have the stars."

"You don't think it's-," Cooper paused while he searched for the right words "-romantic in a western sort of way?"

It was silent as Yancy thought on that.

"Long as you don't mind the snakes, rain, cold, heat, spiders, thorns, dust, ice, and wind - I reckon it might be romantic," he finally said.

Cooper sighed and turned over in his bedroll.

126

"You're hopeless," he said.

"Night," Yancy replied.

Chapter forty-one

The herd moved along with no problems for a week.

Big Spring and Sweetwater were now behind them, and they were getting close to Abilene. The country was mainly wide-open, with small rolling hills and grass a-plenty.

Rondo rode in from scouting. It was midafternoon, and he was scowling.

He rode over to the chuck wagon and drank some water from the water barrel.

"What's the matter?" Tussle asked from the wagon seat.

Rondo nodded towards the north.

"See those clouds? We might be in for a rough night."

"I've been watching them," Tussle nodded. "Mebbe they'll go to the west."

"Too early to tell," Rondo said, and suggested, "There's a big lakebed full of rainwater a few miles ahead. Might be best if we stopped and settled the herd early, just in case."

"Sounds good," Tussle nodded.

"I'll tell the others," Rondo said.

He started to lope off. But, before he could, they spotted Cooper, who was riding point, loping towards them.

"What's he doing?" Tussle asked.

"Must be trouble," Rondo replied.

Everybody gathered around him as he came up, and Lee trotted up from the remuda.

"I saw Injuns," Cooper announced. "They're coming over that hill yonder."

"How many?" Tussle asked.

"A dozen or so."

Before anybody could say anything, three Indians topped out on a hill. They pulled up their horses, and then they just sat there. A few seconds passed, and they held their hands high and started making hand signals.

"Anybody know what tribe they're from?" Tussle asked.

Everyone looked at Josie and waited while she studied them.

"Comanche," she finally said.

"Think they're hostile?" Tussle asked.

"I think not," Josie shook her head.

"Can you make out what they're saying?"

"They are hungry. They want beef."

Lee looked at Rondo and chuckled.

"Does this bring back any memories?" He asked.

"Sure does."

"What are you two talking about?" Tussle snapped.

"Same thing happened last time Lee and I were on a cattle drive," Rondo explained. "Come to think on it, we were driving your cows too."

Tussle grunted.

"I remember," he said, and asked, "What happened?"

"These two Injuns wanted some steers for beef, but Kinrich killed them."

"What happened after that?" Yancy spoke up.

"A lot more Injuns showed up," Rondo said.

"And in a hurry," Lee added.

The Indians continued to make hand signals, and Rondo looked at Tussle.

"We'd best give them an answer," he said.

Tussle scratched his stubbled jaw in thought.

"I hate to lose 'em, but I reckon we'd better give them a few head," he decided, and added, "I noticed a few cripples at the back. Cut them out."

"Will do," Rondo nodded.

"Coop, you and Joise go talk to them," Tussle said. "Yancy, you help Rondo."

"Sure thing," Yancy nodded.

"And everybody else had better get back where they belong before we lose the entire herd," Tussle added sourly.

Everybody nodded and moved out.

Chapter forty-two

Cooper checked his Colt, and then he and Josie rode up the hill and pulled up in front of them.

The Indians were older, tired looking, and rode scrubby looking mustangs. The rest of the Indians waited at the bottom of the hill, and Cooper spotted a few women and children in the bunch.

The oldest looking Indian started jabbering in Comanche. Josie spoke back sharply, and all three Indians were shocked. They glanced at each other, and the oldest one spoke up again.

Josie listened and talked back, and the Indian grunted his approval.

"Comanches are powerful hungry," Josie told Cooper. "I told them we will give them a few head."

"Good," Cooper nodded.

Suddenly, the old brave burst out a long line of Comanche. While he talked, he pointed to the east.

Josie listened carefully, and she turned to Cooper with a worried look.

"He wants to repay our kindness with a warning," she said.

"What warning?"

"Two days ago, they came across a bunch of riders. They asked for food, but these men shot at them and killed two Indians. He said they are very bad men."

Cooper pinched his face in thought.

"How many were in this bunch?"

Josie asked, and said, "Ten or so."

Cooper nodded thoughtfully and looked at the old Indian.

"'Preciate it," he said.

The Indian nodded, and Cooper and Josie turned their horses and rode back down the hill.

130

***

Yancy was sullen as they cut out three crippled yearlings.

"I've been watching that steer all day," he pointed. "He wouldn't have made it much further."

"Looks like it," Rondo agreed.

"Sorta hate to see him go," Yancy said.

"Why's that?"

"I was hoping for a steak for supper."

Rondo smiled, and they drove the steers up the hill.

Soon as they reached the top, the Indians took them and moved aside to butcher them.

"They ain't wasting any time," Yancy commented as they rode back down the hill.

"They're hungry," Rondo replied.

"So am I," Yancy grumbled.

***

Everybody looked thoughtful when Cooper told them what the Indian had said.

"Do you think it's the bunch that attacked us?" Jessica asked, her eyes wide with fright.

"Could be," Cooper said.

"What are we going to do?"

"Nothing we can do at the moment," Tussle spoke up, and he glanced at the fast building clouds. "We'd better get the herd moving. Looks like a storm's coming."

They spread out and got the herd lined out. Rondo led them to the lakebed, and they bedded down the herd and got prepared for the storm.

Lightening played across the sky as they ate supper, and there was also a cool breeze picking up.

131

"I want Jessica, Josie, and Wyatt to stay in camp tonight," Tussle said. "But everybody else had better stay with the herd. Lee, you and Brian stay with the horses."

Wyatt looked disappointed as everybody stood. They saddled up fresh mounts and rode out.

It started sprinkling as they spread out around the herd. Then the raindrops got bigger, and it fell in sheets.

It was a cold, piercing rain, and the cattle turned their backs to it.

Even with the lightening, the yearlings were in no mood to go anywhere. They bunched together as tightly as possible and dropped their heads.

The horses didn't like the cold rain either. And, despite everyone's efforts, the horses put their backs to the hard rain and wouldn't budge.

After that, there was nothing to do but hunker down in the saddle.

It rained steadily for two hours, and everybody got soaked. Then the breeze picked up even more, and it turned cold.

Yancy and Cooper were close to one another, and Yancy could see him shivering in the saddle.

"Feeling romantic yet?" Yancy shouted at him.

Cooper scowled, and his reply was lost in the rain.

Chapter forty-three

It couldn't get daylight fast enough.

The firewood was wet, and it took Tussle a while to build a fire.

Once it was going, he and Wyatt stayed on the other side of the chuck wagon while Josie and Jessica undressed and dried their clothes. They switched as soon as they were dry and dressed.

Soaked cow-punchers started drifting in, and they took turns drying their clothes and eating breakfast.

This took a while, and it was midmorning before they got the herd lined out and moving.

Rondo rode over to Tussle.

"Think I'll ride out and scout for that other bunch," he said.

"You be careful," Tussle said.

"Will do," Rondo said, and he trotted out.

***

It was late in the morning when three men approached the herd from the south.

Yancy and Cooper saw them coming, and they all met at the chuck wagon.

They were a rough looking bunch. One was tall, one was short, and the other was burly.

"Afternoon," the burly man said. "My name's Albert, and these are my brothers. We spotted your herd, and thought we'd see if you needed any help."

Tussle looked thoughtful as he looked them over.

"Which way you boys headed?" He asked.

"Nowhere in particular," Albert shrugged.

Yancy and Cooper felt an instant distrust of the men, but their faces remained emotionless.

Tussle didn't trust them either. However, he was worried about the bunch that the Indians had seen, and he wanted as many men as he could muster in case of trouble.

"You boys ever punch cows before?" He asked.

"We've been up the trail a time or two," Albert replied.

"All right," Tussle decided. "We'll take you on."

"'Preciate it," Albert grinned.

Tussle deliberately split them up.

"Albert, you ride point, and you ride drag," he instructed the short one, and then he looked at the tall one. "You ride on the right flank, in front of Yancy."

They nodded and kicked up their horses.

Soon as they were gone, Tussle glanced at Yancy and Cooper.

There was no need to say anything. They understood to watch them, and they nodded and took out.

The herd moved on out, and the rest of the morning passed uneventfully.

Chapter forty-four

Jessica rode behind Cooper that afternoon, and she looked to be in deep thought.

The country they were in had a lot of grass, and the yearlings were in no hurry. They grazed as they walked, and they had to be pushed along.

Tussle went on ahead around midafternoon to set up camp, and Josie went with him to help.

Cooper stretched in the saddle. He stopped, stepped off his horse, and tightened his cinch. Jessica came up beside him as he climbed back on, and he smiled at her.

"How is Jessica today?" He asked.

"Tired," she smiled wryly. "I didn't get much sleep last night."

"Nobody did," Cooper said as he rode beside her.

"But, it was a good time to think," she added.

"Oh? What about?"

"Your brother. He's hard to figure out."

Cooper grinned, and his white teeth shown at her.

"Yes, ma'am. He is."

"Has he always been this difficult?"

"Pretty much."

"What was he like when you two were children?"

"Shorter."

Jessica laughed.

"Yes, I imagine he was," she said.

It was silent, and a wistful look crossed her face.

"Things didn't go so well the other night," she admitted.

"I noticed that," Cooper said, and asked, "What went wrong?"

"Well, it started when Yancy mentioned Lee."

"He's never liked Lee."

"I don't either. Not anymore."

Cooper shot Jessica a quizzical look.

"What happened between you two?"

Jessica explained about the hotel, and how Lee lost it.

"But then Yancy told me that the hotel is half mine again," she said. "I was excited, but Yancy looked disappointed."

Cooper smiled faintly and nodded.

"You don't need him," he said softly.

"How's that?" Jessica looked confused.

"Mind if I get personal?"

"What have we been doing so far?"

Cooper grinned briefly. He took in a deep breath, let it out, and cleared his throat.

"Your wealth intimidates Yancy. It makes him feel not good enough, like he can't support you. And that means a lot to Yancy."

Jessica pinched her face in thought, and she looked at Cooper and frowned.

"That's it?"

"Yep, that's it."

"So," Jessica talked it out. "If I'm poor he likes me, but if I'm rich he doesn't?"

"That's one way to look at it."

"Your brother is very peculiar."

"Yes, ma'am."

"Still, in an odd way, that's sort of sweet."

Cooper looked at Jessica and raised an eyebrow.

"It is?"

"Yes," Jessica decided, and her face lit up with admiration. "It is."

"Personally, if Josie had money, I wouldn't mind it so much. Might even like it."

"Yes, but Yancy wants to take care of me," Jessica reasoned. "And, if I'm rich, he can't take care of me as well."

"That's it," Cooper nodded, and added, "Long as I've known him, he's always felt compelled to take care of everybody. That's why he's such a good lawman."

"He loves being a Texas Ranger, doesn't he?"

"He does."

"And I tried to talk him out of it," she admitted.

"I wouldn't do that, if'n I was you."

"I won't," Jessica said. "Not anymore."

"So, what's next?" Cooper looked at her.

"Well, I'll catch him in a good mood and talk to him if I can," Jessica said, and added, "My only problem is, I can never tell what mood he's in. He's so quiet."

"Watch his hands," Cooper instructed.

"His hands?"

"Sure. If he's holding a gun," Cooper explained, "he's probably mad."

Jessica laughed. A few seconds passed, and she looked at Cooper and grinned.

"It's too bad," she said.

"What is?"

"You and I get along so well," she pointed out.

"I reckon we do," Cooper agreed.

"If only Yancy and I got along this well," she said wistfully.

Cooper smiled as he thought on that.

"If we wanted to get married," he explained wryly, "mebbe we wouldn't get along so well either."

137

Chapter forty-five

From across the herd, Yancy watched as Cooper and Jessica talked. Then Jessica laughed whole-heartedly, and he felt a tug of jealously.

They finally separated, and Jessica trotted back to the remuda to change horses.

Yancy grunted his displeasure as he started to turn around in the saddle.

Soon as he moved, he heard a loud buzzing from a rattlesnake beneath him. His horse was spooked, and he jumped to the side.

Yancy was thrown sideways, and his spur accidentally jobbed the horse in the flank. The horse squealed, and he dropped his head and started bucking.

The jumps were high and big.

Yancy managed to stay in the saddle for the first two jumps. On the third jump, the horse sucked backwards, and Yancy did a flip in the air and landed hard on his back. The breath was knocked out of him, and all he could do was just lie there.

Cooper saw the bronc ride, and he trotted around the drag and came up behind him.

Yancy was still lying there, gasping for air.

"You all right?" Cooper asked.

Yancy groaned.

"I feel like my innards have been seriously disarranged."

"I've never seen a man flip quite like that."

"It's a special talent," Yancy moaned, and he grimaced as he sat up.

Several feet away, the buzzing sound returned.

Yancy forgot about his aches and pains. He jumped to his feet and moved sideways.

"Kill that snake, will you?" He said sourly.

Cooper smiled and dismounted.

***

Lee spotted Jessica riding toward them, and he glanced over at Brian.

"Here comes trouble," he said.

Brian nodded in agreement as she trotted up.

"Jessica," Lee said.

Her face was stern, but she managed to nod.

"Lee."

Lee looked at Brian.

"Cut her out a gentle one," he said, and Brian took off.

Jessica dismounted and started unsaddling her horse.

"Here, I'll do it," Lee offered.

"Thank you," Jessica replied stiffly, and she handed Lee her reins.

Lee felt her eyes on him as he worked, but he remained silent.

Brian trotted up with another horse. Lee bridled him, and he swung the saddle blanket on, followed by the saddle. He tightened the cinch and turned towards Jessica.

"Here you go," he said as he handed her the reins.

"Thank you."

Lee nodded and started to turn away, but Jessica just stood there and looked at them.

"Do you need anything else?" Lee asked.

"I talked with Yancy," she said.

Lee's face lit up.

"So you know about the hotel?"

"I know."

"Good," Lee said, and Brian nodded. "That's all we wanted."

"I don't want it," she said suddenly.

"What?" Lee looked confused.

"The hotel. I don't want it."

Lee glanced at Brian and looked back at her.

139

"Mind explaining that a little?"

"It's simple. I just don't want it."

"But we went through a lot, and I mean a lot, getting that hotel back," Lee pointed out.

"Well, you shouldn't have."

Lee was flustered, and he stood there a moment as he thought on it.

"But it's yours," he finally objected. "Jeremiah's expecting to hear from you."

"But I don't want it. I have my reasons."

"What are we supposed to do with it then?"

"You and Brian can have it," Jessica said. "Do whatever you want with it."

"Just like that?" Lee stared at her.

"Just like that," Jessica said, and she climbed on her horse and looked down at them. "I wouldn't expect either one of you to understand."

"I'm glad, because we don't," Lee laughed shakily.

Jessica nodded and kicked up her horse. She traveled a few feet, but then pulled up abruptly.

"I'm sorry I've been so rude," she apologized. "I want to thank you both for helping my Uncle. He really appreciates it."

Lee and Brian nodded, and she kicked up her horse again.

They watched her leave, and then they looked at each other.

"Well! I sure didn't see that coming," Lee said.

"Me neither," Brian agreed.

"I don't think I'll ever figure Jessica out," Lee said.

"I don't want to even try."

"Now that I think on it, neither do I," Lee smiled.

"Well, looks like we're back in the hotel business," Brian commented.

Lee thought on that, and his smile turned into a grin.

"It does, don't it?" He said.

140

Chapter forty-six

After the rattlesnake was dead, Cooper caught Yancy's horse and led him over to him. Yancy took the reins, and he scowled as he climbed back on.

"You all right?" Cooper asked.

"I'm fine," he muttered, and asked, "What were you and Jessica talking about?"

Cooper was surprised.

"You saw us?"

"'Course I did," Yancy growled. "What was she laughing about?"

"I don't think I should say," Cooper said as he stepped into the saddle.

"Why not?" Yancy glared at him.

"It was personal."

"For you, or her?"

"I'd say both."

Yancy scowled, and Cooper smiled.

"You ain't gonna tell me," Yancy said.

"Nope."

Yancy grunted, and they kicked up their horses and rejoined the herd.

A few seconds passed, and Yancy sat up straight in the saddle.

"Albert's gone," he gestured at the point.

"So is Sim," concern filled Cooper's face.

They looked behind them, and the other two hands were missing too.

"This ain't good," Yancy said.

"I wonder where they went?"

"Tussle," Yancy's voice was grim. "He went on up ahead to set up camp."

"And Josie's with him," Cooper reminded.

"Let's go," Yancy declared.

"Shouldn't we fetch Lee and Brian?"

"I don't think we have the time," Yancy said matter-of-factly.

Cooper nodded, and they kicked up their horses.

Chapter forty-seven

Rondo rode east in a brisk trot. He kept his eyes peeled for tracks, but he also scouted the grass and water for the next few days.

By evening time he was miles from the herd, and darkness overtook him as he rode back to the west.

A few hours back, Rondo had passed a lakebed with a tank full of water.

He was approaching the lakebed again when he suddenly smelled campfire smoke.

He pulled up, dismounted, and tied his horse to a mesquite bush.

"You stay here," Rondo whispered. "And keep quiet."

He pulled out a pair of well-worn moccasins from his saddlebags, pulled off his boots, and pulled them on. Next, he checked his Colt, and he crouched down and took off.

Josie would have been proud. His feet made the slightest sound through the tall grass, and he was nearly invisible.

There were some trees ahead, and Rondo made his way over to them. He could hear voices now, and he crouched even lower as he crept from tree to tree.

He could see the light of a campfire in front of him. He got down on his knees and crawled through the brush. He gained a good vantage point of the camp, and he was so close that he hardly dared to breath.

He counted seven men lounging around the fire.

All were hard looking men, and he almost jumped when he recognized Butch Nelson and Rock Bullen.

This is the bunch that attacked us, he figured.

Harsh words interrupted his thoughts.

"Listen, Rock, I don't mind your suggestions, but I'm running things. And so far, your suggestions haven't worked out too well."

143

"Give Sim and Albert a chance," Rock replied patiently. "They'll get Tussle."

"They could be dead by now."

"We don't know that."

"Well, either way, we'll be prepared tomorrow," Butch declared.

"What do you have in mind?"

"Before you reach the lakebed, there's a steep ridge on both sides," Butch said. "It makes sort of a natural corral."

"I saw that."

"If things go as planned, Albert will lead the Landons here. The top of those ridges would be the perfect spot for an ambush."

"Seems like," Rock agreed.

"But, if things go wrong," Butch continued, "they'll show up here tomorrow with the herd. And, seeing how there's good water, they'll probably camp here."

"Sounds reasonable."

"We'll be waiting on the ridges," Butch declared. "Once they're down in the bottom, we'll have 'em trapped. We'll pick Tussle off and be gone."

"That might actually work," Rock grudgingly admitted.

"'Course it will," Butch grunted, and added, "In the morning we'll scout the ridges, and find us a few good spots to hide."

They talked some more, but Rondo had heard enough. He crawled backwards through the brush, and as soon as he could stand he trotted back to his horse.

Rondo untied him, stepped into the saddle, and wasted no time getting back to Tussle's camp.

Chapter forty-eight

There was a small hill ahead, and from the top Yancy and Cooper could see the chuck wagon's canvas top. There were also several horses scattered around the wagon.

"There they are," Yancy said.

"Something's wrong down there," Cooper said, and he pulled out his rifle from his scabbard.

"We go loping up, and it could make things worse," Yancy figured.

Cooper nodded, and they dismounted and tied their horses to some nearby bushes. Then, they crouched low and trotted towards the chuck wagon.

As they came down the slope, Yancy spotted Josie and Tussle. They were standing rigid at the back of the wagon.

Then he saw Sim and the three new hands. They were standing directly in front of Tussle and Josie, and they covered them with their rifles.

Yancy glanced at Cooper. He saw them too, and his face was grim.

They could hear voices as they made their way to the front of the wagon.

"Do what you want with me," Tussle was saying. "Just let Josie go."

Albert snorted.

"You don't understand," he said harshly. "We're taking over the herd."

"You'll never accomplish that," Tussle fired back. "Don't you know who you're up against?"

"We'll see about that," Albert sneered.

Sim spoke up.

"We're wasting time," he said impatiently. "Let's kill Tussle and get out of here."

"All right," Albert said, and a soft click sounded out as he pulled the hammer back on his rifle.

145

"Don't be an idiot," Sim said harshly. "Kill him silent like. We don't want them hearing us."

"You're right, I wasn't thinking."

Yancy took a quick peek around the wagon.

He saw Albert give his rifle to Sim, and he pulled out a bowie knife and walked towards Tussle.

Tussle stood his ground, and a hard look crossed his face.

"Let's go," Yancy said quietly, and he and Cooper walked forward.

"Hold it," Yancy said sternly.

The four outlaws were startled as the Landons walked around the chuck wagon. Sim's eyes grew wide, and he took a few steps backwards, but that was all.

Yancy breathed easy as he watched them. No words were spoken, and the silence was tense.

Suddenly, Albert made a grab for his Colt, and the other outlaws lifted their rifles.

With an easy motion, Yancy palmed his Colt and fired. His first two shots hit the small man, and he screamed and flew backwards.

Cooper fired one shot after another into the tall man. As he crumbled over, he managed to fire one shot harmlessly into the ground.

Tussle's new Winchester was leaning against the chuck wagon, and he dove for it. He grabbed it and rolled over into a sitting position while bullets flew over his head.

Albert stood directly in front of him, and a wicked snarl was on his face as he took aim. But, before he could fire, bullets from Yancy's six-shooter and Cooper's rifle hit him in the chest, and he was flipped over backwards.

In the confusion, Sim almost dropped his rifle. But then he recovered and took aim at Cooper.

Before he could fire, Josie pulled her knife from her sheath and let it fly.

146

The knife struck him in his shoulder, and he screamed and stumbled backwards. He dropped his rifle as he ran wildly for his horse.

Yancy and Cooper turned to fire at him, but then they realized that their weapons were empty.

They were helpless as Sim jumped on his horse and took out in a dead run.

A thought suddenly occurred to Cooper, and he turned to Tussle.

"Give me that Winchester."

Tussle handed it to him.

Using his thumb, Cooper pushed his hat back and lifted the Winchester to his shoulder. He squinted, took in a deep breath, aimed, and pulled the trigger.

The rifle boomed loudly, and everybody watched as Sim rode on.

"Missed him!" Tussle observed.

Cooper grunted his displeasure. He worked the lever, took in another breath, aimed, and fired again.

A few seconds later, Sim fell from the saddle.

"Got him this time!" Tussle exclaimed.

Cooper frowned as he gave the rifle back to Tussle.

"Shoots a mite to the left," he said.

***

A few minutes later they heard the pounding of hooves, and Lee and Brian stormed into camp. Jessica and Wyatt were close behind.

There was no need for explanations. They studied the dead bodies, and then Lee asked, "Is everybody all right?"

"I think so," Cooper said.

"Looks like we have more graves to dig," Lee said, and everybody nodded.

Chapter forty-nine

By the time Rondo got back to camp, it had been dark for several hours. His horse was lathered in sweat, and Rondo looked worried.

"'Bout time you got back," Tussle grunted as he dismounted. "Where you been?"

Rondo didn't reply as he glanced around camp.

"Where's Sim? Is he with the herd?"

"No, Wyatt and Josie are with the herd. Sim's dead."

"What happened?"

Tussle told him, and only then did Rondo relax.

"I found their camp," he announced, and he told them all that he'd heard.

"So Butch Nelson is behind all of this," Yancy said thoughtfully.

"Him, and Rock Bullen."

"I wonder what Butch is after?" Yancy asked.

"I don't know, but he sure wants Tussle dead."

"Why?" Tussle wanted to know.

"I didn't ask," Rondo smiled faintly.

"How far is this lakebed?" Yancy asked.

"Several miles."

"And they're camped there now?"

"Sure are," Rondo said, and asked, "You thinking what I'm thinking?"

"They're right where they want us to be," Yancy replied, and Rondo nodded.

"What do you have in mind?" Tussle spoke back up.

Rondo explained his plan. Afterwards, everybody looked at Tussle, and he nodded.

"Let's do it," he declared, and added, "I want Wyatt, Jessica, and Josie to stay with the chuck wagon."

"That would be best," Cooper agreed. "I'll tell Josie and Wyatt."

Rondo caught a fresh horse while everybody else saddled up, and then Cooper went to fetch Josie and Wyatt.

While they waited, Jessica walked over to Yancy.

"Can we talk?" She asked. "Alone?"

Yancy studied her and nodded.

"Make it quick," he said.

They walked to the outskirts of camp, away from the others.

"I want to apologize," Jessica said.

"For what?"

"For being so pushy the other night."

Yancy smiled softly.

"Mebbe I need to be pushed."

"No, I was wrong," Jessica said, and added, "Cooper and I had a talk."

"Yes, I saw that."

"He explained a few things to me."

"He did, did he?"

"Don't be upset," Jessica said quickly. "I see things completely differently now."

"What things?"

"For starters, I lost the hotel again."

Yancy was startled.

"How did you manage that?"

"Lee and Brian have it now."

"We'll see about that," Yancy muttered.

"No, you don't understand. I gave it to them."

Yancy was flustered, and he stared at her with his mouth open.

"Why'd you do that?"

"That hotel was built with money I inherited from my father's plantation," Jessica explained, and added, "I wish I'd never inherited all that money. All it's caused me is grief. I've been kidnapped, taken hostage, dragged across New Mexico, cheated, and shot at because of that money."

"You have been through a lot," Yancy smiled faintly.

149

"And I'm ready to move on to better things. That's why I gave the hotel to Lee and Brian."

Yancy was silent as he thought on that.

"What better things do you have in mind?" He asked.

She smiled, and the look on her face said it all.

Yancy smiled back, but then his face got dark.

"You need to hear this now," he said. He gathered his thoughts, and said, "I can't offer you the life you're accustomed to living. Not on my salary."

"You mean the life I'm living now?" Jessica smiled playfully. "Out on the trail, living with men and no baths?"

Yancy smiled at that.

"I reckon these last few days have been rough. Especially for women folk."

"You don't see me complaining."

Yancy studied her thoughtfully.

"No, I don't."

Cooper, Josie, and Wyatt rode in from the herd, and everybody else climbed on their horses.

"Well, you'd better run along and do your job," Jessica said, and added, "Be careful."

Yancy nodded. He stepped up on his horse and looked back down at her.

"We'll be back," he said, and he kicked up his horse and joined the others.

Chapter fifty

It took some persuasion to get the bedded down yearlings up and moving. Rondo took the point, and the others spread out behind him.

The moon was full, and it was a light night. The yearlings became restless, and they had to circle them several times to keep them together.

They reached the lakebed just before midnight.

Rondo spotted the two ridges, and he pointed the herd towards the opening.

He motioned at the others, and pistol shots popped from behind as Brian and Cooper scattered a few shots over the yearling's heads.

The frustrated herd surged ahead. As one unit, they broke into an all-out run.

***

Rock sat up, startled. Butch was sitting up too, and they frowned.

A dull rumble sounded like thunder in the distance.

"What is that?" Butch asked.

Rock didn't reply, and his Colt was in his hand as he stood.

Butch stood tense, listening hard, and he could hear distant pistol shots.

Everybody else was awake now, and they stood there looking confused.

"What's going on?" A sleepy outlaw asked.

"I'm not waiting around to find out," Butch replied. "Let's get out of here."

Panic broke out as everybody pulled on their pants and shirts and dashed to their horses.

151

Rock and Butch were ahead of everybody else, and they were the only ones saddled when the yearlings surged into view. They were in a dead run, coming straight towards their camp.

On each flank were several riders, and whining bullets peppered the camp.

Rock and Butch fought with their frightened horses as they swung on, and they left in a dead run.

A searching bullet flew by Butch's head, and he ducked down as they raced forward.

Meanwhile, the other outlaws were stranded as their terrified horses broke and ran.

There was nothing to do but make a stand. They fired one shot after another as the swirling mass of yearlings raced through their camp.

One bearded outlaw jumped sideways. He took one step, grabbed at his chest, and went down.

Another outlaw rolled around on the ground, grabbing his leg. He screamed as the herd flattened him.

Two other outlaws were firing at the running horsemen. But their shots weren't close, and as the herd came at them they panicked. They started to turn and run, but before they could one fell from a bullet and the other one was trampled.

The last outlaw in camp managed to grab a horse. But the horse was terrified and wouldn't stand still as he tried to step into the saddle. The horse jumped sideways, and he lost his grip. He fell backwards, and his foot slipped through the stirrup.

The frightened horse took out in a run, dragging the screaming, helpless rider behind.

***

Rondo pulled up his horse and reloaded. Yancy, Cooper, Lee, Tussle, and Brian came up beside him and did the same.

152

"Two got away," Rondo said.

"I saw them," Yancy nodded. "Soon as it gets daylight, we'll go after them."

Everybody nodded and nudged their horses forward.

The outlaw camp was in shambles. There were four bodies spread about, plus a horse.

They dismounted and looked around.

Rondo walked over to the outlaws, and he was surprised to find the youngest one still alive. He was on his back, grasping his belly.

"Help me, please," he said in a whimper.

The others walked up as Rondo knelt by him.

"Not much I can do," Rondo said as he looked him over.

"I'm dying?" The young outlaw asked as a thin stream of blood ran from the corner of his mouth.

"Looks like it," Rondo nodded, and asked, "You want to talk?"

"'Bout what?" He gasped.

"Why were you boys trying to take the herd?"

The young outlaw seemed anxious, even eager, to talk. He told them everything, even about Lucy Wells, and he also told them what little he knew about the railroad.

Afterwards, everybody glanced thoughtfully at each other.

"We'll make you comfortable," Rondo told him. "You have any folks to notify?"

The young outlaw nodded and told him where his parents lived.

"We'll tell them," Yancy spoke up.

"Tell them I'm sorry," he said. "For everything."

153

Chapter fifty-one

After their talk with the wounded outlaw, Yancy, Cooper, and Tussle took off to fetch the chuck wagon and the others. Rondo rode out to see what he could find, and Lee and Brian built the fire back up and straightened up the camp.

The young outlaw died as Tussle arrived with the chuck wagon. He started breakfast while everybody else dug graves.

Rondo rode back in a little while later.

"They're headed south," he announced as he dismounted.

"See any of the stock?" Tussle asked.

"Some," Rondo nodded. "I don't think they scattered out too bad. Plenty of grass out there. Most of them stopped to graze."

"Soon as we eat breakfast, we'd better scatter out and see what we can gather back up," Tussle said.

"I'm sorry, Tussle, but Coop and I are going after Rock and Butch," Yancy spoke up. "This is Texas Ranger business now."

"I'm going with you," Lee declared.

"You'll need a good tracker," Rondo put in.

"And I ride with Lee," Brian added.

"Now hold on," Tussle protested. "Somebody's got to stay with the herd."

Nobody said anything as they looked at each other, and Tussle took charge.

"Rondo, you've been leading this drive, so you've got to stay. And Coop, you belong with your family. Brian, you're as old as I am. You should stay with the remuda."

Nobody looked happy, but they still reluctantly agreed.

"That only leaves me and Lee," Yancy spoke up.

154

"That's right," Tussle agreed. "And Lee's a good tracker."

Yancy glanced at Lee, and they didn't say anything as they looked at each other.

"We'd best be going," Lee finally said.

"All right," Yancy replied. "Let's go."

While everybody watched, they walked over to their horses and stepped into the saddle.

Jessica looked worried, and Yancy smiled down at her.

"We'll be back," he said.

"I know you will," she said.

Yancy nodded, and he and Lee kicked up their horses and trotted out.

"Should be interesting," Rondo said as they watched them.

"What's that?" Cooper asked.

"Them two, riding together."

Cooper nodded thoughtfully.

"Could be," he agreed.

Tussle was impatient.

"All right, let's get going," he urged.

Rondo, Cooper, Brian, Wyatt, Josie, and Jessica mounted up and rode out of camp. They spread out and made a big gather, and by late afternoon they drove what they had found back to the lakebed.

Cooper and Wyatt stayed with the herd while everyone else rode to the chuck wagon.

Rondo dismounted and poured himself a cup of coffee.

"Looks like we got lucky," he told Tussle. "Roughly speaking, I'd say we only lost a couple hundred head."

"That's better than I had hoped for," Tussle looked pleased.

"We could look around some more tomorrow," Rondo offered.

"No, we've wasted enough time already," Tussle said, and asked, "How close are we to Fort Worth?"

155

"Pretty close. But, spread out as we are, it'll probably take us a couple days to get there."

"There's always the chance somebody might ride up, looking for a job," Tussle suggested.

"I hope not," Rondo smiled.

Chapter fifty-two

Butch and Rock didn't speak as they traveled south in a brisk trot.

They rode through the night, and come daylight they slowed their horses to a walk. Only then did they speak.

"Well, that didn't work out too well," Rock commented.

"They knew we were there," Butch growled.

"I'd say so."

"Those Landons are annoying."

"And good shots," Rock added.

"I can't figure why Lee Mattingly is riding with them," Butch said. "Everybody knows he and Yancy can't stand each other."

"Mebbe they worked out their differences."

Butch grunted, and they trotted on.

"Speaking of differences," Rock said. "There's one thing I can't figure."

"What's that?"

"You already got a fine ranch, and I also saw how Lucy was smiling at you," Rock explained, and asked, "Why are you picking a fight with Tussle when you got all that waiting for you?"

"Been wondering that myself," Butch admitted. "Ike always said he wanted all he could get. I reckon I did too."

"And now?"

"That ranch in Empty-lake looks mighty good. Mebbe even Lucy."

"You'll also need a partner," Rock said suddenly.

Butch looked sideways and studied him.

"Meaning you?"

"Sure. Why not?"

"I thought you were a bounty hunter."

"I don't have to be," Rock shrugged. "Mebbe I'd like to settle down."

"With me and Lucy?"

"Well, mebbe later I'd find me someone," Rock smiled.

Butch frowned but didn't say anything.

"You'll need someone like me," Rock continued. "I have connections."

"So do I."

"But not like I have," Rock said, and explained, "We'll need cattle, and I can get 'em real cheap."

"How?"

"Are we partners?"

Butch thought on it and sighed.

"Fine," he agreed.

Rock smiled and nodded.

"Good," he said.

"You should know," Butch said. "Lucy wants you dead."

An amused look crossed Rock's face.

"There's gratitude for you," he said. "She's the only prisoner I never killed."

"I'll talk with her, and change her mind."

"I'd appreciate that."

Butch nodded, and it was silent for a bit.

"Well, it'll take us a few weeks to get back to Empty-lake," Butch commented after a while.

"We've work to do first," Rock said.

"What's that?" Butch asked, confused.

"They'll be following us."

"I figured they'd be too busy gathering the herd back up to worry about us," Butch disagreed.

"It's the Landons," Rock said matter-of-factly. "They never give up."

Butch frowned thoughtfully and nodded slowly.

"You might be right," he said, and asked, "How do you suggest we handle it?"

"It'd be real easy to set up an ambush."

"Think they'd fall for it?"

"Only one way to find out."

Butch nodded.

"Well, we'd best find us a good spot and hide the horses," he said.

"Reckon so," Rock agreed.

Chapter fifty-three

The morning passed uneventfully for Yancy and Lee.

Lee leaned over the saddle horn, following the tracks, while Yancy watched the surrounding landscape for anything suspicious.

"What are we gonna do when we catch them?" Lee asked around midday.

"Arrest them," Yancy declared.

"What if they don't want to be arrested?"

"You know that answer."

Lee grinned.

"I reckon I do," he said, and added, "I just wanted to be sure. This is my first time to ride with a Texas Ranger."

"This is my first time to ride with an outlaw," Yancy grunted.

"You mean a pardoned outlaw?"

"For now."

Lee narrowed his eyes.

"What do you mean by that?"

"I'm confident you'll mess up again, one of these days."

Lee scowled.

"I appreciate your confidence."

"Anytime," Yancy replied, and it fell silent.

The afternoon wore on. The tracks continued due south, and the country got rougher. There were more trees, with lots of ridges and steep hills.

"They've slowed down some," Lee gestured at the tracks.

"Horses must be tired," Yancy suggested.

"That, or they want us to follow them."

"Good point."

There was a cluster of trees in front of them. Past the trees, the ground sloped upwards to a rocky ridge.

The tracks went to the side of the trees and then went upwards.

"A feller could get ambushed in country like this," Yancy commented as they approached the trees.

"Sure could," Lee agreed.

"Be almost impossible to avoid it, unless one of us went up ahead on foot."

"But that would slow us down."

"Be better than dying."

"I can see your point."

Yancy gestured ahead.

"Let's climb that ridge and see what's on the other side. We'll decide from there."

"Sounds good," Lee nodded.

They rode by the trees and into a flat clearing. The ridge was steep, but there was an old cow trail that led to the top.

There were just starting to climb when a rifle shot boomed out. There was a loud thump as a bullet hit flesh, and Lee's horse stumbled.

Lee managed to throw himself from the saddle as his horse fell, and he landed in a heap beside him.

Yancy dove off his horse. While in midair he drew his Colt, and as he hit the ground he fired up the slope. His shots were close, and he heard a surprised yell.

Yancy's horse was spooked, but Lee jumped up and grabbed his reins before he could take off. Then, while Yancy fired one shot after another up the hill, Lee led the horse to safety behind the trees.

Yancy heard a clicking sound as he emptied his six-shooter. He turned and ran wildly for the trees while bullets rained down all around him.

He was about to reach the trees when he felt a sharp tug on his shoulder. He lost his balance and hit the ground rolling. He came up on his feet and dove behind the trees.

Lee, meanwhile, tied Yancy's horse to a tree branch and hunkered down behind a tree.

"Hit bad?" Lee asked.

Yancy took a quick look at his shoulder.

"No, he just nicked me."

"Good," Lee looked relieved.

Rifle shots from up above sounded out, and bullets bit into the bark of the trees. Yancy and Lee ducked, and then Lee fired back.

"Hold your fire," Yancy said as he peeked upwards. "There's no way we can get 'em from down here."

"So we just lie here and take it?"

"No, but if we leave these trees, they can pick us off in any direction," Yancy pointed out.

"We need to flank them," Lee declared.

"That'd be nice, but there's no way we can climb that ridge. It's too open."

Lee pinched his face in thought.

"All right," he drawled, and he nodded at Yancy's horse. "Climb on him and get outta here."

"And leave you here?" Yancy frowned distastefully.

"Sure. You'd probably like that."

Yancy frowned but didn't say anything.

"I'm serious," Lee looked over at him. "Get on your horse and git."

"You want to explain that a little?"

"If you leave now, they'll figure I'm dead," Lee said.

"It's possible."

"They'll also come down to inspect their kill," Lee continued. "When they do, I'll be ready."

"You'll take on both of them?"

"Yep."

"They're both good. Real good."

"So am I."

Yancy pinched his face in thought.

"I don't feel right, leaving you here."

"Can you think of anything better?"

"We could stay here 'til dark and then leave."

"But they'd get away," Lee disagreed. "And, we can't catch them with just one horse."

They had to hunker down as more shots came from above, and several of the bullets ricocheted dangerously amongst the trees.

"Get going before they bounce a bullet in one of our guts," Lee growled.

Yancy still didn't like it, but he reluctantly agreed.

"I'll ride over that hill behind us," he gestured. "I'll stop there."

"Sounds good," Lee nodded. "Now get going."

Yancy nodded and holstered his Colt.

He looked like he wanted to say something, but instead he sprang to his feet and ran for his horse. He jumped into the saddle and kicked up his horse.

His horse needed no encouragement. They broke into a run, and bullets rained down around him as they made their escape. The horse never broke stride, and soon they were out of sight.

The shooting from the ridge stopped, and Lee hunkered down behind his tree.

"Come to Papa," he said softly.

Chapter fifty-four

Several minutes passed, but to Lee it felt like hours.

He lay perfectly still, and he closed his eyes as he listened for approaching footsteps.

He finally heard them, and they were talking as they came down the slope.

"I got a good look with my spyglass," Butch was saying. "It was Lee and Yancy. Yancy left, so Lee must be dead."

"I sure thought it was Yancy I hit," Rock replied.

"He didn't look hurt when he was riding out."

"No, he didn't," Rock agreed, and added, "Least now we can collect that reward."

"Long as he's dead, I don't care."

Keeping behind the cover of the trees, Lee crawled sideways. Then, he crept from tree to tree as he went in a circle.

He could still hear their voices as they searched for him.

"He's got to be around here somewhere," Rock said.

"Look at that tree. There's a bit of blood," Butch replied.

"But where is he?" Rock asked, irritation in his voice.

Lee straightened up and walked towards the voices. He could see them now, their backs to him as they searched for him.

"Looking for me?" He asked softly as he stepped out into the open.

Their bodies stiffened, and they stood there rigid.

"Turn around. Real slow," Lee ordered.

They did, and both smiled when they saw Lee. He was just standing there, and his Colt was holstered.

"We meet again," Lee looked at Rock.

"Where's your fishing pole?" Rock smiled wolfishly.

"Don't need one at the moment."

"That was a nice trick, getting us down here," Rock said.

"It worked."

Rock laughed, but not humorously.

"Now what?"

"Well, you could always surrender."

"No, don't think we will," Rock's eyes twinkled.

"I figured that."

"You think you're good enough, to take us both?" Rock asked.

"Yes."

Rock grunted, and it fell silent.

Lee just stood there, his hand hovering over his Colt handle, and watched their eyes.

Several long seconds passed, and Lee's heart thumped in anticipation.

Rock suddenly blinked and grabbed for his Colt, as did Butch.

With an easy movement, Lee palmed his Colt.

Rock was good, and he cleared leather. But, before he could fire, Lee shot him in the chest. He staggered backwards and crumpled over.

Lee turned and shot Butch.

Butch had cleared leather too, and his first bullet fanned air close to Lee's head. But then Lee's bullet struck him in his midsection.

He grunted and took a step back. He tried to raise his Colt, but another bullet from Lee hit him in his torso, and the impact flipped him over backwards. He landed on his back, kicked out, and was still.

Lee's face was emotionless as he looked at them.

He took in a deep breath and let it out slowly. He opened the cylinder of his Colt, took out three spent shells, inserted new ones, closed the cylinder, and holstered his Colt.

He heard the pounding of hooves, and he turned and watched as Yancy loped towards him.

Yancy pulled his horse up abruptly, and it was silent as they looked at each other.

"You all right?" Yancy finally asked.

165

"Better than them."

"I watched through my spyglass," Yancy commented. "If you'd shot Butch first instead of Rock, he might of won."

"But I didn't," Lee smiled.

Chapter fifty-five

They made camp that night about a mile from Fort Worth.

The next morning, John Lythe and several hands rode out to the herd. Rondo saw them coming, and they met at the chuck wagon.

"You made it," John smiled a big, easy grin.

"We did," Tussle nodded.

"Have any trouble?"

Tussle glanced at Rondo and looked back at John.

"None that we couldn't handle," he said.

"You made good time," John commented as he looked at the herd. "They're in good shape too."

"They could be better," Tussle replied gruffly.

John smiled and nodded.

"We'll take good care of 'em," he declared.

The contract changed hands, and he motioned at his men to take the herd. Then, he looked back at Tussle and grinned.

"Why don't you take your crew into town and freshen up?" He suggested. "You've earned it."

"No, we'll be heading back now," Tussle replied. "There's work to be done."

"I can understand that."

"I'll be expecting to hear from you in a few months," Tussle said.

"Yes, sir. Just as soon as we get back."

Tussle nodded and said, "Well, good luck."

John said goodbye and kicked up his horse. Meanwhile, Rondo rounded up his crew, and they watched as John's crew took over.

"Well," Rondo commented. "There they go."

"Be a long drive to Kansas," Cooper added.

Everybody nodded, and they rode to the remuda and spread out. They might not have yearlings anymore, but there were still the horses to take back to the ranch.

They covered several miles before stopping time. Tussle set up camp, and it was mostly quiet during supper.

Jessica sat beside Cooper, and she looked worried.

"I hope nothing happened to Yancy," she said wistfully. A few seconds passed, and she added, "And Lee."

"They'll be fine," Cooper reassured her.

"When should they be back?"

"Things like this take time. Don't worry. They'll be along."

Cooper's words didn't bring her any comfort, and she frowned as she ate her beans.

Chapter fifty-six

It took several hours to bury Rock and Butch.

After that, Lee pulled his saddle off his horse while Yancy fetched the two outlaw's horses. Lee saddled Rock's horse, and they mounted up. Lee led the extra horse as they trotted along.

They traveled several miles before darkness hit, and they made camp in a dry gully. They didn't have any coffee, so they just sat there and ate some canned goods.

"I almost miss Tussle's beans," Lee commented.

"I don't."

Lee chuckled. It was silent for a moment, and he cleared his throat.

"While we have a moment, there's something we need to discuss."

"Oh? What?"

"Jessica."

Yancy stiffened.

"What about her?"

"We've both been fond of her for a long time," Lee declared. "We both know it."

"I reckon we have."

"I had always hoped-," Lee's voice trailed off, and he shrugged.

"And now?" Yancy asked, and he couldn't help but sound anxious.

"Feelings change, I reckon."

"How so?"

"I still like her, just not that way," Lee explained, and added, "Besides, you two deserve each other."

"What do you mean?"

"You're both stubborn and hard to get along with."

Yancy scowled, but didn't reply.

"Anyhow, I wanted you to know that," Lee continued. "You don't have to worry about me anymore."

"I never was."

"Sure you wasn't."

It fell silent as Yancy thought on that.

"There's somebody else, isn't there," he finally said.

Lee was startled, but then a wistful look crossed his face.

"There is," he admitted.

"What's the holdup?"

"Me."

"I should have known."

"I wouldn't be talking, if'n I was you. You ain't no Don Juan either."

"No, reckon not," Yancy smiled faintly.

Lee grunted and pulled out a cigar. He bit off the end, struck a match, lit the cigar, and took a deep puff.

"Soon as we get back to the ranch, Brian and I are headed to Empty-lake," Lee spoke up. "Rondo will probably come along too. He's got to fetch Rachel."

Yancy nodded but remained silent.

"Did you hear about the hotel?" Lee asked.

"Yes, Jessica told me."

"I can't figure out why she gave it to us."

"It's complicated."

"Well, whatever the reason, I'm a respectable businessman again."

"Looks like."

"And, soon as you get me that pardon, I'll be free to go wherever I choose," Lee said. He paused and added, "I could settle down, if'n I wanted."

"You could."

"Sure is something to think about."

Yancy nodded, and Lee took a deep puff on his cigar.

"Would you mind if Coop and I rode with you to Empty-lake?" Yancy changed the subject.

Lee shot Yancy a questioning look.

"Why are you two going to Empty-lake?"

"Lucy Nash."

"Oh? What about her?"

"We're going to arrest her and put her back in Huntsville," Yancy explained.

Lee grinned wolfishly at the thought.

"Have you ever met her?" He asked.

"No, I haven't had the pleasure."

"It's always an interesting experience."

"I'm sure it will be," Yancy smiled.

Chapter fifty-seven

The next day was torture for Jessica.

She kept searching the landscape as they rode, looking for any sign of them. The day passed slowly, and her fear grew with each passing hour.

They had just stopped to make camp that evening when she spotted two riders in the distance.

"There they are!" She exclaimed.

Everybody looked, and a relieved expression crossed Cooper's face. They all stood as they rode up, and Yancy and Jessica stared at each other.

"You get 'em?" Tussle asked.

"We did," Lee nodded.

"Good," Tussle looked pleased. "Climb on down. You're just in time for supper."

They tended to their horses and walked up to the chuck wagon. Jessica noticed the dried blood on Yancy's shirt, and she uttered a small cry.

"You're hurt!"

"Naw, it's just a scratch."

"I fix?" Josie offered.

"No, no," Yancy said quickly. "I'm fine."

Josie shrugged and walked away.

"You sit down and rest," Jessica took over. "I'll get you your food."

"Beans?" Yancy asked.

"Yes."

"Can't wait."

He walked away from camp a bit and settled down. Jessica joined him a few minutes later, and it was silent as they ate.

"I was so worried," Jessica finally said.

"You shouldn't have been."

172

"I couldn't help myself," Jessica said, and added, "I've never been so sweaty in my life."

"Heat must be getting to you," Yancy looked at her, concerned. "Perhaps you should ride in the wagon tomorrow."

"It wasn't the heat."

"Oh? What was it?"

Jessica took in a deep breath and let it out.

"Are you planning on marrying me?"

Yancy was startled, and he almost dropped his plate of beans.

"Marriage?"

"I don't mean to be pushy. I'd just like to know."

"Well," Yancy looked flustered. "Don't you think we should get to know each other a little more first?"

"You don't believe in love at first sight?"

Yancy thought on that, and a sheepish grin crossed his face.

"I reckon it does save a lot of time," he said.

"And a lot of conversation," Jessica added.

"That it does," Yancy agreed. It was silent for a moment, and he added, "Tell you what. Coop and I have to go down south and arrest Lucy Nash. When we get back, we'll finish this conversation."

"I'm looking forward to that," Jessica grinned.

Epilogue

They arrived back at the ranch several days later.

Tussle offered for Josie and Wyatt to stay at the ranch while everybody went south, but Josie objected.

"I go with you," she told Cooper.

"I know you want to," Cooper smiled gently, "but you're needed here. Tussle won't have any help until he can find some new hands."

Josie frowned and crossed her arms.

"How long will you be gone?"

"Three or four weeks."

"That is a long time."

"We'll survive," Cooper smiled.

"Just hurry," Josie demanded.

"Yes, ma'am," Cooper's eyes twinkled.

***

They rode out the next morning.

They saddled their horses after breakfast, and Tussle, Jessica, Josie, and Wyatt stood on the porch and watched them as they led their horses out of the barn.

While Cooper said goodbye to Josie and Wyatt, Yancy just stood there and looked at Jessica. Their eyes met, and Yancy smiled.

"I'll see you when we get back," he said.

Jessica nodded and said, "Be careful."

"We always are," he said, and added, "Most of the time."

Jessica smiled and shook her head as everybody climbed on their horse.

"I want to thank you boys," Tussle spoke up, and his voice was husky. "For everything."

174

Cooper glanced sideways at everybody, and then spoke for them all.

"It's what we do," he said.

Tussle nodded, and he looked genuinely moved.

Cooper looked once more at Josie, and Yancy looked at Jessica. Several seconds passed, and Yancy turned his horse. Lee fell in beside him, and Rondo, Cooper, and Brian followed. Cooper led Jug-head while Brian led No-see-ums.

Tussle leaned against the porch railing as he watched them trot out.

"There's a sight I thought I'd never see," he said.

"What's that?" Jessica asked.

"Yancy and Lee, riding together."

A thoughtful look crossed Jessica's face, and she nodded slowly.

"They rode together," she said.

Author's note

The Chisholm Trail led to the new profession of trail drive contractors. Some of the larger ranches delivered their own stock, but trail drive contractors handled the majority of herds going to Kansas. Among them were John T. Lytle and his partners. John T. Lytle took over 600,000 head of cattle up The Chisholm Trail between the years of 1871 and 1887.

About the Author

Born in West Texas, Tell Cotten is a seventh generation Texan. He comes from a family with a ranching heritage and is a member of the Sons of the Republic of Texas. Besides writing, he is also in the cattle business, and he resides in West Texas with his wife, Andi, and their two children.

Tell has enjoyed writing from an early age, and he also has a great love of the history of the west. THEY RODE TOGETHER is his seventh novel in The Landon Saga series.

For announcements of new releases and all other information, please like The Landon Saga Page on Facebook https://www.facebook.com/TheLandonSaga Or, you can join The Landon Saga Fan Group https://www.facebook.com/groups/784798154926122/ You can also visit Tell Cotten's website http://tellcotten.wordpress.com/

Acknowledgements
I would like to thank my wife and my family for all their help and support. Without them this wouldn't be possible. I'd also like to thank God for the gift of writing.

Special thanks goes out to Bill for the fantastic drawing, and thanks to Marcy and Mike for putting the cover together.

And lastly, I'd like to thank Melissa for all her advice, help, and hard work.

Enjoy this excerpt from Tell Cotten's upcoming novel:
Warpath
Book eight in The Landon Saga series

Rondo pulled up his horse abruptly and leaned forward in the saddle.

"What is it?" Lee asked as everybody stopped behind him.

"The tracks come together again."

Lee scratched his jaw in thought.

"That's odd. I wonder why they split off?"

"I'm not sure."

"Mebbe one of them died, and they went to bury him," Brian suggested.

"Yancy and Coop will figure it out," Rondo said, and he glanced up at the sun. "Be dark soon. Might as well make camp and wait for them."

Everybody agreed, and they dismounted and took care of their horses.

"I'll gather some firewood," Jeremiah Wisdom offered.

"Don't go too far," Rondo cautioned him.

Jeremiah nodded and took out, and Brian went with him.

Rondo and Lee set up camp, and then they waited for firewood.

Lee sat and leaned against his saddle. He pulled out a cigar, bit off the end, struck a match on his saddle horn, lit the cigar, and took a deep puff.

His face looked thoughtful as he exhaled.

"Been thinking," he said.

"You usually do," Rondo replied.

"You have Rachel, Cooper has Josie, and Yancy has Jessica."

"If she's still alive."

"We can't think that way," Lee frowned at his friend. "Rachel's alive, and so is April."

A wistful look crossed Rondo's face.

"She'd better be."

"Josie lived with the Apaches," Lee reminded. "I remember her saying they wouldn't kill women or kids unless they had good reason."

"Josie would know."

"She sure would."

Rondo nodded, and it was silent for a bit.

"If we get through this, I'm gonna ask for April's hand in marriage," Lee suddenly said.

Rondo turned and studied Lee with a thoughtful look.

"It's about time," he said.

"She's a good woman," Lee continued. "And, June's a good kid."

"I'd say so."

"We'd get along just fine. And, now that I'm back in the hotel business, I also have something to offer her."

"I don't think she cares what you have to offer. She just wants you."

Before Lee could reply, they heard the sound of a horse.

"Here they come," Rondo said, and they stood.

Jeremiah and Brian walked in with armfuls of firewood as Yancy trotted up to their camp. His face was grim.

"Where's Cooper?" Rondo asked, confused.

"He'll be along."

Rondo nodded and asked, "Find anything?"

Yancy nodded somberly.

"Back in the rocks," he said softly. "We found a body."

"An Injun?" Lee spoke up.

"No, it was a woman," Yancy replied. He paused and added, "A white woman."

Nobody spoke, and the silence was heavy. Both Lee and Rondo's face were drawn tight.

"Was it Rachel?" Rondo finally asked, his voice husky.

"Couldn't tell," Yancy said. "We don't know who it was."

"What do you mean?" Lee demanded.

179

Yancy sighed, gathered his thoughts, and continued.

"She was scalped, and her body was all cut up and swollen. From the looks of it, she's been dead for a day or two."

"What about her clothes?" Rondo asked. "Rachel had a yellow dress-."

Yancy looked uncomfortable.

"She wasn't wearing anything," he said, and added, "Cooper stayed to give her a decent burial. I came on ahead to find you."

"I'm going back," Lee demanded. "I can recognize her."

"I'm going with you," Rondo and Jeremiah declared.

They started towards their horses, but Yancy stopped them.

"No," he said, and his voice was hard and cold. "It wouldn't do any of you any good. I tell you she's unrecognizable. Don't ask me to explain it anymore than that."

"But we've got to know who it is," Rondo objected, and his voice almost broke.

"We catch those Apaches, and we'll know."

Rondo looked at Lee. Several long seconds passed, and they walked back to camp and sat down sullenly.

"All right," Rondo vowed. "We'll catch them, if it's the last thing I ever do."

Lee and Jeremiah nodded their agreement.

Coming soon from Solstice Publishing

For announcements of new releases and all other information, please like The Landon Sage Page on Facebook https://www.facebook.com/TheLandonSaga or you can join The Landon Saga Facebook group https://www.facebook.com/groups/784798154926122/